NANA EKVTIMISHVILI

TRANSLATED FROM THE GEORGIAN
BY ELIZABETH HEIGHWAY

Peirene

მსხლების მინდორი

AUTHOR

Nana Ekvtimishvili, born in 1978 in Tbilisi, Georgia, is a writer and film director. She studied screenwriting and drama at Potsdam-Babelsberg. In 2013, with her partner Simon Groß, she directed the feature film *In Bloom*, which premiered at the 63rd Berlinale, where it won the CICAE Award. It went on to win numerous awards at festivals in Hong Kong, Tokyo, Paris, Los Angeles and Sarajevo, and was also selected as Georgia's entry for the 2013 Academy Award for Best Foreign Language Film. The International Federation of Film Critics said it heralded a 'rebirth for Georgian cinema'. Her latest film, *My Happy Family*, was released at the Sundance Film Festival in 2017. Published in 2015, *The Pear Field* is Ekvtimishvili's first novel. It was awarded the Ilia State University prize for the best Georgian novel published in 2014-15; the Saba Literary Prize for best debut; and the Litera Prize, also for the best debut, given by the Writers' House and the Ministry of Education, Science, Culture and Sport of Georgia. It has already been published in German and in Dutch to much critical acclaim.

TRANSLATOR

Elizabeth Heighway has worked as a translator from Georgian and French since 2010. She has translated a number of contemporary Georgian works, including Aka Morchiladze's *Journey to Karabakh* and the anthology *Contemporary Georgian Fiction*, both published by Dalkey Archive Press.

NANA EKVTIMISHVILI

TRANSLATED FROM THE GEORGIAN
BY ELIZABETH HEIGHWAY

Peirene

The Pear Field

First published in Great Britain in 2020 by
Peirene Press Ltd
17 Cheverton Road
London N19 3BB
www.peirenepress.com

First published in 2015 under the original Georgian-language title მსხლების მინდორი
by ბაკურ სულაკაურის გამომცემლობა, Tbilisi, Georgia

ISBN 978-1-908670-60-1

Designed by Sacha Davison Lunt
Cover image: Ryan Searle / Unsplash
Typeset by Tetragon, London
Printed and bound by TJ Books Limited, Padstow, Cornwall

The book is published with the support of the Writers' House of Georgia.

**WRITERS'
HOUSE
OF GEORGIA**

Supported using public funding by
**ARTS COUNCIL
ENGLAND**

1

On the outskirts of Tbilisi, where most of the streets have no names and where whole neighbourhoods consist of nothing but Soviet high-rises grouped into blocks, grouped in turn into microdistricts, lies Kerch Street. There's nothing worth seeing here, no historic buildings, no fountains, no monuments to society's greatest accomplishments, just tower blocks lining both sides of the street and, now and then, another building tucked between them: the College of Light Industry, up on the plateau surrounded by spruce trees; the kindergarten; the municipal middle school; the offices of the housing management committee; a small shopping centre; and, at the very end of the street, the Residential School for Intellectually Disabled Children or, as the locals call it, the School for Idiots.

Nobody can remember whose idea it was, back in 1974, to name a street in Soviet Georgia after a town on the Crimean peninsula; a town where, one sunny day in October 1942, as the summer breeze carried the warmth of the Black Sea waters inland, the Nazi army stormed the quarry and took several thousand prisoners. There are no ships here. There's no breeze coming in off the sea. It is late spring and the sun is oppressively hot, drawing up steam from the tarmac and wilting the tall maples. Occasionally a car rolls by and a dog might haul itself up from where it is sprawled on the road and bark, until the car turns off and the dog has nothing to do but gaze after it, disconsolate, before going back to rolling in the dust.

Kerch Street boasts no heroes, unlike its namesake. As Nazi forces rounded up the citizens of Kerch, Jews and non-Jews, ten thousand besieged Soviet fighters mounted a brave and selfless defence. In the end they were defeated. Maybe that is why, after the war, the Soviet authorities chose not to make Kerch a 'Hero City'. Their decision meant the city would receive no state aid; instead, it would have to rebuild under its own steam. Only in 1973 was Kerch awarded the title 'Hero City'. A year later, the first section of road from Tbilisi to Tianeti was renamed Kerch Street. One by one, the local men who had lived through the Great Patriotic War passed on: men who had strolled out on public holidays with their medals pinned to their jackets; slow, dignified men, puffing out their thin chests as they walked up and down in the sunshine; men who hung Stalin's photo on their living-room walls. When their time came, they entrusted the fatherland to their children and grandchildren, who still live on or around Kerch Street today, going back and forth between their homes, kinder-gartens, schools, shops and jobs, their whole lives contained in this neighbourhood. When the Soviet Union fell, their lives were blown apart. Some residents took refuge within the four walls of home. Others came out of their houses and passed their time on the street corners instead, or spent hour after hour at rallies or on picket lines. Some took down those photos of Stalin from their living-room walls. Some simply gave up the ghost.

On a sunny day in late spring, in the wash block of the School for Idiots, stands Lela, head bowed under a stream of hot water, thinking.

I have to kill Vano…

Lela, who turned eighteen a month ago, lives at the school.

I'm going to kill Vano, and then they can do what they want with me.

Lela turns off the tap. Steam rises from her thin, flushed body. Her spine is clearly visible in the middle of her back, running like twisted cord from her narrow waist to her shoulders.

I'm going to kill him, she thinks, threading her arms through the sleeves of her khaki-coloured shirt and buttoning it up. Next to her stands a classroom chair, its yellow wood split and softened by the humid air. There are slivers of laundry soap and a half-toothless comb on the seat, and clothes hanging over the back. Lela pushes her legs into her trousers, tucks her shirt in and pulls her belt tight.

They won't lock me up though, will they? They'll just say I'm crazy. Or backward… Worst-case scenario, they send me to the madhouse. That's what they did with Tariel's lad and look at him now, walking around as free as a bird…
She runs her fingers through dripping hair and shakes her

head like a wet dog. Just then the door of the wash block opens with a bang and Lela sees a small, hazy silhouette appear through the steam.

'Are you in here?' Irakli calls, standing at the door. Lela carries on getting dressed, forcing her wet feet into her socks. 'Dali's been looking for you everywhere!'

'What does she want?' Lela puts on her trainer and pulls the laces tight. The breeze coming through the open door has cleared the steam and she can see Irakli now, even his pointy ears and wide eyes. He sighs.

'Just hurry up, will you? Dali wants you… They're on the trampolines again, and they won't come down.'

Lela laces her other trainer and hurries after him.

It's sunny and warm outside. They run across the deserted playground that connects the long, single-storey wash block and the dormitory building.

Lela dresses like a boy and at first glance she looks like one too, especially when she's running flat out. Up close, though, you can see her fine, fair eyebrows, her dark eyes, slim face and cracked red lips, and under her shirt the swell of her breasts.

'Dali can't get them out. They're on the bed bases,' Irakli says, panting heavily.

They clear the wide steps outside the entrance in one leap and run in through the door.

The air in the large tiled foyer is cool, as always. There are empty display cabinets on the walls and a red fire extinguisher fixed alongside.

Lela runs up to the top floor and down the long corridor. She can hear Dali's whining voice coming from the room at the end. She runs in to find a large group of children darting around and jumping on the mesh bed bases. There's a deafening *squeak-squeak-squeak*. In the middle is a short, plump woman who at first glance seems to be playing tag with the children but failing to catch anyone. This is Dali, the school's Head of Discipline, who is also acting as supervisor today. She has dyed red hair so thin you can see her scalp. It sticks out in every direction, framing her head like the halo on a saint's icon and in fact, with the suffering she goes through chasing these children all day, she could be the school's patron martyr-saint.

It's only a few months since the Ministry gave the school 'humanitarian aid' in the form of new wooden beds. The heavy, decades-old iron beds they replaced were dismantled and carried up to a room on the top floor. The ceiling leaked even when children used to sleep there. Builders repaired the ceiling, but it started leaking again. They fixed it a second time, and a third… but every time it rained, the rain leaked through until everyone came to accept that that's just how things were. Now, whenever it rains, the children run up to the room to watch. There are buckets and jugs placed all over the floor to catch the water so it can be thrown back out of the windows. The room is now known as the trampoline room and no matter what Dali does she can't keep the children out: nothing in that school comes close to the sheer joy of jumping on bedsprings, especially in the rain.

The room has recently gained one more attraction: without warning, its little balcony collapsed, sending lumps of concrete crashing down into a pile on the ground and taking with it the iron guard rail and a number of roofing slates. Now there is just a length of supporting beam sticking out of the wall. No one was hurt, even though the playground was full of children playing football at the time. Needless to say, the school authorities were so relieved they barely had time to be annoyed that the balcony had collapsed in the first place. But a few days later the door leading out to the balcony vanished too, as did its frame. Whoever took it probably reasoned that, as the balcony no longer existed, nobody would need the door leading onto it. So now there's a door-sized void in one wall of the trampoline room through which, on days like today, you can see a cloudless blue sky, poplar trees and the block of flats next door.

'Get out! Out, or I'll put you over my knee!' screams Dali as the children chase each other around, laughing. She notices Lela. 'You see? I tied the doors shut with wire and they still got in and now look. Total bedlam!'

Lela spots Vaska standing in the corner. Vaska is a Lom, an Armenian gypsy, fifteen years old and small for his age. He's lived here a long time. Lela remembers when he first arrived. He was eight, she was eleven. He was brought by his uncle, a dark-skinned man with green eyes and hairy, tattooed arms who was smoking a cigarette. The man never came back. At first Vaska hung around Lela, who took him under her wing and kept him safe from the other children, for whom newcomers were little more than fresh prey. Then, when they were slightly older, they had sex. Neither of them saw it coming. It happened outside the wash block, under the pear trees, at the edge of a waterlogged field. That night, Lela recalls, the playground suddenly emptied. Dali was watching some South American soap opera about a young woman's tempestuous relationship with her mother-in-law. Having never missed an episode, she'd managed to get most of the children hooked too. That night they'd all gone inside to watch, leaving Lela and Vaska alone in the playground. Lela can't remember exactly how it happened. She remembers them walking out to the pear trees. She remembers them taking their clothes off. It didn't hurt like it had before. In fact, it felt tender and careful. *He* felt tender and careful... The only thing she didn't like was the feel of the bones in his pelvis. They kissed on the lips. Vaska already knew how to use tongues. They didn't say a word. Not the first time, nor later when they met again and again under the pear trees. Lela can't quite remember when things changed. She can't remember when or why she started to dislike Vaska or why she began putting him down. He never stood up to her. Even now he calmly takes whatever she throws at him. In fact, he smiles. Lela hates that smile. She's itching to fly at him, to punch that rosy-lipped smile right off Vaska's face. He's always smiling. It was different when he first arrived at the school. He was more talkative then. He never stood apart from the others, never stared off into the distance like he does now. He didn't have that smile permanently plastered on his face. It appeared out of nowhere, an ambiguous, slightly disdainful smile that leaves you wondering whether he's smiling to himself, or mocking you, or not really smiling at all.

'Why are you just standing there, idiot?' Lela snaps. 'Can't you give Dali a hand?'

Vaska looks at Lela with his light green eyes and that smile on his face and says something under his breath.

Lela heads over to where the balcony used to be. Two children are standing right on the sill and one, six-year-old Pako, a daring new arrival in black shorts and a Mickey Mouse T-shirt, has ventured out onto the iron beam like a tiny smiling tightrope walker.

'What did I tell you?' Lela screams suddenly. 'I told you not to come over here! Just wait till I get my hands on you!'

The two children make a run for it. Pako teeters unsteadily, but manages to regain his balance by holding his arms out, then carefully inches back along the narrow beam towards the doorway. Lela grabs him by the back of the neck before he's even in the room and lets him dangle. Pako's face crumples and drains of colour. His legs thrash in mid-air.

'Shall I let go? Shall I?'

Lela gives him a shake. Pako reaches desperately towards her.

'Shall I let you fall? Is that what you want? Splat on the ground with a broken neck?'

Lela pulls him inside and lets go. Pako scuttles off like a wind-up toy beetle.

'Wait till I get my hands on you lot!' Lela shouts.

Irakli herds the children out of the room. Vaska is nowhere to be seen. The last child, Stella, runs off on weak, bowed legs, bottom sticking out behind her, dressed in only thick woollen leggings with a turtleneck jumper tucked into her waistband. Lela, Irakli and Dali stay behind. Her halo in disarray, Dali sits down hard on one of the bed frames, buckling the iron mesh with her weight and almost falling through onto the floor. Irakli grabs her flailing hands and helps her back up to perch on the edge. She gives a deep sigh.

'Irakli, find Tiniko and ask whether she could *possibly* lend me that padlock she's been promising me for *goodness* knows how long so that we can put it on the damn door before one of them falls out, because a *fat* lot of good it'll do then…'

Irakli runs off. Dali wets her hands in a bucket of rainwater and wipes her brow.

'I can't take this any more,' she groans, and then shouts after Irakli, 'If you see any of the others, tell them to go straight to the dinner hall!'

Lela stands in the empty doorway and looks down. She imagines herself shoving him out: Vano, the elderly history teacher and current deputy head. The shove takes him by surprise. He stumbles, trips backwards on the sill, feels the void beneath him… He stares up at Lela, eyes wide behind his glasses, and sees in her face not a hint of concern that he is plunging down from the top floor. And his own face crumples, just like Pako's, and he stares, wild-eyed, as she spits out, 'Die, you fucking bastard!'. He slams into the pile of concrete below and rasps his final breath.

'Here's the lock,' she hears Irakli say. She turns. Dali has gone.

'She said Dali should lock it and give her the key. This one doesn't work, though. She got it off the letter box...'

Lela takes the tiny lock from Irakli.

'This won't keep *anybody* out,' she says.

But they leave the room. Lela closes the door, locks it with the little padlock and gives the key to Irakli. Then she tests the lock, giving the door a tug using about as much strength as she thinks Stella would.

They walk down the corridor side by side. Irakli comes up to Lela's shoulders. Lela lights a cigarette. Stella runs out of one of the rooms looking startled, with no idea where she's supposed to be going.

'Dinner hall, now!' Irakli says, and Stella runs off.

They make their way down the stairs.

'Will you take me over to use the phone?' Irakli asks.

'You really are an idiot, you know that? Just let it go! Stop making a fool of yourself!'

'She said this week, though. I swear to God!'

They go out into the yard. In front of the building is a wide asphalt forecourt where, as usual, Avto, the PE teacher, has parked his light blue van. The rest of the yard is bare earth covered in spruce needles.

They walk over to the dinner hall, cutting across the small open space between the main dormitory block and the administration building, where lessons take place and where Tiniko, the school's director, has her office. A relatively well-maintained two-storey building, it has windows where there are supposed to be windows, and balconies to boot.

Ten-year-old Sergo comes striding out with something pink and knitted tucked under his arm. Kolya emerges behind him, dragging his feet, bobbing his head. You'd be hard pushed to guess how old Kolya is; he could be ten, he could be fifteen.

You can tell Kolya's slow, thinks Lela. *Sometimes you can tell, sometimes you can't. You can't tell with Sergo or Irakli.*

'Dinner hall, now!' shouts Irakli. 'Dali said! Sergo! Kolya!'

Sergo ignores Irakli, but Kolya hesitates, then sets off back towards the dinner hall.

'Where are you going?' Lela asks Sergo.

He walks straight past her and heads towards the main gates. 'Kiosk!' he says, without turning round.

'What for?'

'Tiniko told me to take this dress back.'

He pulls the pink knitted fabric from under his arm with a magician's flourish, then turns round to show Lela. She eyes him mistrustfully. Sergo laughs.

'Don't you believe me?' He holds the dress up against his body. 'Looks great on me, doesn't it?'

'Yeah. Watch no one kidnaps you!' Lela says, laughing, and carries on towards the dinner hall.

Sergo stands there for a minute patiently folding the dress and then runs out of the front gates to cross over to Zaira's kiosk. It's not the first time Tiniko has returned clothes like this. Zaira's sister-in-law brings cheap clothing over from Turkey and Zaira sells it alongside other bits and bobs.

The smell of fried potatoes and onion, mingled with an indeterminate rancid stench, reaches Irakli and Lela as they near the dinner hall. Lela takes a last drag of her cigarette and throws the butt to the ground, then spins round on hearing a muffled bang and the screech of car brakes out in the street. She peers through the spruce trees. Irakli is already running towards the gate. Tariel, a middle-aged man with a limp who wears an old sheepskin jacket whatever the weather, staggers out of the gatehouse, tries to run and falls over. Lela hears loud wailing. She runs outside.

Emerging from the shade of the spruce-lined yard, Lela is hit by the street's fierce heat. The midday sun casts slender, trembling shadows at the feet of the few who have ventured out. Nearby a car lies half on, half off the carriageway. A man gets out, dazed and unsteady, and hurries off, leaving the car door open. Tariel and Irakli run after him and Lela follows. She sees Sergo, thrown across the edge of the pavement, immobile. Another car pulls up, the door slams and someone walks quickly across the tarmac. Did Sergo just twitch? People are speaking at once: 'I was driving along... He just ran out in front of me... I'm a doctor... Somebody call an ambulance...'

Tariel and Irakli touch Sergo gently.

'Sergo!' Irakli cries. 'Serozha!'

They roll Sergo onto his back. He is covered in blood.

'Serozha!' Lela touches him lightly on the shoulder.

A man she doesn't recognize pulls her roughly to one side, kneels down next to Sergo, presses two dirty fingers against his soft, delicate neck and stares into the distance, motionless. The man smells foul; his half-open shirt reveals a distended, florid belly, bloated from too much vodka. Lela imagines it's a dagger he's pressing against Sergo's neck to prevent him divulging a secret. Sergo isn't moving. He's not scared of the dagger, nor of the people crowding around him. The man's secret is safe with Sergo.

Zaira comes running out of her kiosk, beating her fists against her head. Everyone has questions: 'Who is he?... Who let this child go outside?... What happened?'

Tiniko is standing by the school gates. Well dressed as always, she is wearing a short black skirt, shiny black high-heeled shoes and a green frilly blouse. She comes over as fast as her heavy legs can carry her, a black gemstone necklace swaying back and forth with her breasts as she runs. She is as white as a sheet. Lela catches isolated fragments of conversations: '... an ambulance... CPR... he came out of nowhere... I was driving along and he just ran out...' Tiniko looks down at Sergo and the blood on the tarmac. Her face is wild, contorted. The pink dress lies crumpled on the road, pinned under someone's foot, covered in blood.

The men examine Sergo. One says that he's breathing, and a breeze blows in from a nearby garden and somehow calms the crowd. Lela hears a man giving the ambulance driver directions over the phone.

The pavement slowly fills with people, as if somewhere on the other side of this forgotten, sun-scorched street they had been hidden away, waiting for something just like this to lure them out. Suddenly a slim woman notices Zaira faint and calls for water. Zaira sinks to the pavement and sits, slumped, her legs spread immodestly in front of her. Avto, the PE teacher, supports her back with his shoulder. A man barks at the bystanders to give them some air. They lay Sergo on somebody's jacket.

Tariel tells Tiniko, 'We've called an ambulance.'

'Oh, sweet Lord…' she says, ashen-faced. 'How is he? Is it bad?'

'It's really bad,' says Tariel, and walks back to join the men.

'Don't worry, miss,' says a calm bald-headed man with no neck and red cheeks. 'There's no need to panic, they're taking care of him. Let's just stay back and give them some air. Do you want us to look after the child first or her?' He jerks his head towards Zaira, who is starting to come round but is still slumped on the pavement like a drunk.

Tiniko's face and neck are so red and blotchy it looks as if she has measles. She takes a few steps forward, bends to pick up the dress and folds it quickly, making sure not to get blood on her hands. She notices Lela watching her and then hurries over.

'Here,' she says, holding Lela by the arm. 'Take this – careful, though! Run over to my office and put it in my desk drawer. And don't say a word to anyone, no matter what they ask you, OK?'

Lela looks at Tiniko's sweating face. She takes the dress and runs off, as if running might somehow save Sergo. She's running through the spruce trees in the yard when she sees Dali come out of the dinner hall followed by a large crowd of children, all going as fast as they can. Dali looks like a priest leading his flock, until the children stream past her and she is swallowed up by the crowd.

Lela goes into the admin block. Unlike the doors in the dormitory block, Tiniko's office door is upholstered in soft leather with padded panels. Inside, Lela opens the desk drawer. She sees a large half-eaten bar of chocolate. Lela shoves the bloodied dress inside and closes the drawer. The only items on Tiniko's desk are a small, laminated icon of St George propped against the pencil holder, a register and a plant cutting in a tumbler. The top of the desk is covered with a thick sheet of glass under which there's a calendar, a black-and-white photo of Gregory Peck and passport photos of Tiniko's two sons.

Lela goes back out to the street. The ambulance has already taken Sergo away, leaving only a handful of people standing around, immersed in conversation. The district police inspector, Piruz, who has deep-set, sorrowful eyes and a face far too kind for a policeman, is standing off to one side, talking to the car's driver. Tiniko, Dali, Tariel and a few other locals are also there, along with a small group of young men. Among them is Koba, from the neighbouring tower block, who has a thin face, a long nose and an irritated expression. He spots Lela too, but they say nothing.

Some of the school's children are there and, for the first time in their lives, they're doing exactly as Dali tells them, because she is crying. They follow her back over the road and disappear into the yard.

The neighbours are speculating that Sergo got hit by the car when he sneaked out of school to buy an ice cream from Zaira's kiosk and didn't look before crossing the road. Vaska listens as a tearful Tiniko talks to the bystanders. His smile has gone.

'We tell them not to come out here, we tell them again and again,' Tiniko says, 'but we just don't have the *staff*, we've *told* the Ministry... How can Dali possibly watch them every second?... We need *people*! Everyone knows our situation, but they take no notice! Maybe *now* they'll finally send us some staff...'

That evening the news comes through that Sergo is dead.

Next morning the whole school is unusually quiet. Lessons are cancelled.

Sergo's body comes back from the hospital and they lay him out in the gymnasium, a room with iron grilles on the windows on the lower ground floor of the admin block. It's empty apart from a few wooden exercise bars fixed to the walls and some old sports equipment. Every word spreads through the gym like smoke and rolls into the empty corners. The children are seated on long, low benches against the walls, mouthing silently to each other and staring at where Sergo's shrouded body is laid out on Avto's desk.

Outside, with four other men, stands the driver. He has a short neck, made shorter still by his large double chin, and a bulging vein in his forehead. It rather looks as though he might one day overinflate and explode, like an unfortunate toad blown up by a child with a straw.

A small group of women from the neighbouring block are studying the men, trying to pick out the killer. One of them spots him and fixes him with a penetrating stare. The other women stare too, with a degree of respect for the fact that, despite hitting Sergo, he has enough integrity, enough *courage*, to stand here for all to see.

'I heard it wasn't really his fault,' says one. 'And he seems like a decent guy. They were going to go for cheap zinc for the coffin but he asked for wood! He's taking care of the grave too. They were going to bury the lad in a pauper's grave, no headstone, nothing. Anyone else might not even have bothered to find out how he was doing! I mean, it's not as if the police or the boy's parents are going to come after him.'

There's confusion among the school staff, who had assumed Sergo's body would be taken from the hospital straight to the cemetery. Vano and Tiniko come into the gym. Tiniko is still on edge, shoving her hands into her skirt pockets and then pulling them out to gesture while talking to Vano. She glances nervously at Avto's desk, as if there were a ticking bomb on it rather than Sergo's body.

Lela is sitting with the younger children. Stella presses her grubby, frightened face against Lela's arm and mouths silent words at her.

'Is Sergo dead?' she asks, wide-eyed.

Lela gently takes her hand and whispers, 'Yes, he is.'

Irakli, Vaska, Kolya and a couple of others are perched on the bench, trying as hard as they can to catch what Vano and Tiniko are saying on the other side of the gym. Tiniko glances at the children, mutters something to Vano and walks briskly from the hall. Vano tells Avto to get the children out. 'The priest's on his way. When he gets here we're going to the cemetery,' he says, and heads towards the door.

In his agitated state, Vano somehow gets a half-deflated basketball trapped between his feet. He tries to kick it aside but instead almost trips. Eleven-year-old Levan bursts out laughing. Vano kicks the ball angrily out of the way, glowers at the children and stalks off.

Father Yakob arrives at the school in his long black cassock. He has a bushy black beard and dark steely eyes. The children start asking whether Sergo will be going to hell, to the fire and the demons with their whips and canes and red-hot irons. Dali does her best to reassure them, telling them that Father Yakob will perform the rituals needed to send Sergo's soul to heaven.

The priest walks through the school with Tiniko and Vano, blessing the buildings by daubing a cross in holy oil above each doorway. The children trail after him. When they reach the wash block, the priest circumambulates the building, imbuing it with the grace of God and picking up burrs from the undergrowth on the skirt of his cassock as he goes, as if rescuing tiny, downy creatures desperate for salvation.

After the consecration of the wash block the children congregate in the yard to be baptized. There's a deep hush. Even the youngest know that this ceremony will save them from hellfire. In one fell swoop, Dali becomes godmother to every child there. She seems relieved, revived, happy to take on this new responsibility. Father Yakob hands out wooden crosses to the children and they set about looking for bits of string so they can hang them round their necks.

Nobody comes to view Sergo's body, unless you count a handful of neighbours.

A car pulls up carrying a small wooden coffin. An even more sombre hush descends on the school. The children crowd around the gates. Outside, the man who hit Sergo is giving directions to the driver.

'Those kids may be backward, but they know exactly what's going on, see?' says Venera, linking arms with her son. Goderdzi is forty and still single. He stares blankly at the children, then unhooks his arm and walks over to stand with the men.

Every single child is there to see Sergo put into the coffin and carried away. Every child wants to be at the front, to catch a last glimpse of him. Koba comes out carrying two small classroom chairs to support Sergo's coffin, allowing him a final few minutes in the courtyard of his childhood home. The silence is punctuated only by Dali's stifled sobs. Sergo lies in his narrow casket in a suit sewn specially for the occasion, his arms crossed over his chest, a handkerchief tucked under his tiny lifeless hand, as if he might suddenly wish to wipe away a tear. Were Sergo alive, Levan would surely be cracking jokes about his suit or his unnatural pose, but even he is silent now.

The police inspector carries a single wreath onto the bus. The men lift the coffin to their shoulders as if it weighed nothing. Koba kicks one chair over and then the other and for a moment the chairs on the ground look like sacrificial animals, slaughtered in atonement for Sergo's death.

The teachers and other adults start boarding the bus.

Tiniko turns to Lela. 'Are you coming?'

Irakli is glued to Lela's side.

'I am,' Lela replies, 'but the little ones want to come too…'

Tiniko thinks for a moment, then confers with Dali. Dali surveys the children and pulls some of the younger and less able ones out of the group. She points the rest of them towards the bus. 'On you get then, but stay nice and quiet and behave yourselves.'

The children head off, more like excited day trippers than grieving mourners.

On the bus, Lela looks out of the rear window. Dali is standing by the gates with a small group of children: Kolya, Stella, Pako and a few others. Several are crying and clinging to her legs. The bus moves off slowly, belching black smoke, and falls in behind the car taking Sergo on his final journey. The car drives slowly, as if itself borne aloft by a man at each corner.

The bus pulls up outside Avchala cemetery. The sun is beating down.

Gulnara, the practical skills teacher, tells Lela to keep an eye on the children, who stand in a long line, swinging their arms back and forth like Soviet schoolchildren doing marching drills. They start to make their way up the steep path. Lela wonders whether only normal people end up here, or idiots too.

The men set the coffin down beside the open grave. The priest mutters some prayers over Sergo's body. The teachers look spent. The cemetery is scorched and dusty under the hot sun.

Set slightly back from the path next to the cemetery is a long, nine-storey tower block. The right half has been almost completely destroyed. There are only outer walls left now, blackened hollowed shells. Lela can see right through the building and out the other side. At first glance it looks derelict, but then she sees people are still living in the other half: on the balconies she spots laundry, strings of onions, garlic bulbs and saffron crocuses, old pairs of tights full of unshelled hazelnuts stuffed in for storage. And the whole building seems to be listing, as if slowly sinking into the ground under the weight of its remaining inhabitants.

Father Yakob is still praying. The gravedigger carefully peels back the shroud from the top half of Sergo's body. There he lies in his ash-grey jacket, arms folded across his chest, eyes closed, face distended, his skin dark and mottled. The children stare.

The priest finishes his prayers. The gravedigger pauses to let people say their last goodbyes, but Gulnara just gives a quick nod and then a visceral moan when the shroud is pulled back over Sergo's face.

Although Lela knows Sergo is dead, part of her still expects him to protest. But he says nothing, even when the lid is placed back on the coffin, even when the dry clods of earth patter down on the wooden lid. The teachers and children set off down the slope, leaving Sergo with two labourers and a gravedigger, strangers who commit his body to the ground, somewhere on a hill in Avchala.

'Don't look back!' shouts Gulnara, clutching the fence around somebody's grave to keep from losing her footing.

'Why not, miss?' asks Irakli.

'Tradition,' she replies, losing control and juddering down a steep incline. Avto stands at the bottom, holding out a strong, hairy arm for Gulnara to grab.

'Did you hear? Don't look back!' Lela calls to the procession of children weaving their way between the tombstones.

'Why not, Lela?' Irakli asks again.

'I don't really know,' says Lela, jogging down a small slope.

'Yeah, that's right,' confirms Levan, 'you mustn't look back. Once you've buried them you leave them in peace. No more crying either.'

The bus driver sits in the shade of the half-collapsed tower block, quietly smoking a cigarette, waiting for the mourners to return.

2

Lela can't remember when she first arrived at the school. She doesn't know where she was born or to whom, who it was who gave her up or first brought her to Kerch Street. Tiniko knows nothing about Lela's background either. There's nothing she can tell Lela about her parents that might bring her some comfort. Tiniko must have pulled Lela's file out a hundred times; all they know for sure is that Lela used to live at the children's home near the old locomotive works and that when she was old enough for school they brought her here. That is the sum total of Lela's biography.

Sometimes Lela tries to remember the children's home. She can just about recall a woman sitting at a piano, a New Year's party, a cone-shaped hat on her head made from spotted paper with tinsel stuck on and held in place by a thick rubber band under her chin. Sometimes she wonders whether the woman at the piano and the hat with the spots ever existed.

Every time Lela walks in through the school gates a familiar smell hits her. The closer she gets to the dormitory block, the stronger it becomes, and she can feel the school pulling her back into the fold.

On every floor there are toilets at the end of the corridor. The wind blowing in through the broken windowpanes carries their stench deeper into the building, making the entire corridor smell like a station toilet. The bedrooms, TV room and playrooms have their own smell, and no amount of fresh air can flush it out. It's the smell of dirty children, or sometimes of clothes scrubbed clean with laundry soap; the smell of musty linen and hand-me-down bedding; the smell of paraffin lamps and, in winter, wood stoves; the smell of old armchairs and sticky tape covering cracks in the windows and Chinese mallow plants lined up on the sill. Lela knows each and every smell, even though sometimes they all disappear behind the acrid stench of the toilets. When Lela walks in through the gates this same smell gives her an acute sense of sadness. It reminds her of their gatekeeper Tariel's mother. The whole neighbourhood knew her. She stank of wet leather. A hard-working, resilient woman in her youth, she began to grow feeble in both body and mind the day she put on her widow's weeds. With time she forgot her house, her son and her grandchildren, and spent the rest of her days wandering aimlessly along the school fence. Lela thinks of her the minute she sets foot on school grounds; then, gradually, she gets used to the smell and the woman's ghost slips back out of her mind.

There's one place in the grounds that Lela loves precisely because of its smell. The dormitory block has a fire escape, an iron spiral staircase fixed to the outside wall facing the wash block. In summer the sun heats the rusty metal and releases a strange, sweet smell. Lela's loved going up that staircase ever since she was little, even though its tight spiral makes her dizzy as she climbs and turns, climbs and turns, all the way to the top floor.

Although it's outside in the fresh air, the staircase always smells the same. Lela runs her hand along the rail as she climbs and, when she reaches the top, she puts her palm to her nose and finds the smell unchanged. The staircase ends in a small landing overlooking the playground. If Lela leans over the guard rail she can almost grab the branches of the tall spruce trees that grow alongside. She has spent many hours up there on this staircase. Whenever she goes up she pretends that the stairs lead somewhere else entirely, only to have the fantasy shattered upon coming face to face with the solid, doorless wall at the top.

When the rain falls heavily enough to flush the staircase clean, the raindrops make their own distinctive sound as they land on the sun-baked iron before ricocheting off again. When Lela watches the rain lashing down, she imagines Tariel's mother standing there by the fence, soaked to the skin, waiting for the skies to clear so she can turn her black mourning rags to the sun.

The wash block smells of laundry soap, washing powder and damp, mildew-covered walls, and if someone's got nits there's an eye-watering fog of DDT powder too. Lela has her shower at the start of the week. She goes in alone when the laundry's done and the children have all had their baths. When she pulls her unwashed clothes back onto her freshly washed body, it feels as if she's climbing into an old, familiar skin.

The rancid stench of enormous grease-spattered gas stoves permeates the dinner hall, an unremitting smell that varies only according to that day's menu: porridge, borscht, fried potato with onions, or maybe what they call 'fake cutlets', made from stale bread, potato and herbs.

The admin block smells of nothing at all, unless you count the odour of rich leather that comes from the panelled doors, the occasional whiff of an unwashed child on their way to class and the suggestion of Tiniko's perfume. On some of the doors, the leather panels have been slashed open to reveal a soft yellow filling, handfuls of which have been torn off by the children to use in their play.

The gatehouse smells of Tariel. What else could this tiny room possibly smell of? It is filled with his musty clothes, mothballs, the smoke from his papirosa and his dinner.

Between the wash block and the dormitories there's a wide green field covered in small pear trees. Everyone, young and old, stays well away. The trees produce pears every year without fail and everyone stays away from them too, for the lovely green field is permanently mired in water. Whether it's water flooding in from an old broken pipe or rising up from an underground spring, nobody knows. At first glance, the water seeping up through the soil is barely visible. The field looks so enticing, especially to new arrivals at the school, who run out onto the field and then slow involuntarily, ominously, as their feet sink into the waterlogged soil. So the pear trees just stand there with their knotted trunks and tangle of low-hanging branches, alone and forsaken, and every spring they bring forth large, shiny green pears which nobody touches. The pears rarely ripen before the weather turns cold but instead remain rock-hard; those that do ripen never turn sweet but bear the taste of the peculiar groundwater that seeps into their flesh. If climbing the spiral staircase transports Lela to a fantasy world, running onto the pear field fills her with terror, the fear that she might not make it across, as she imagines the branches taking hold, throwing her onto the ground, pulling her body into the soft boggy soil, the roots snaking around her and swallowing her up for ever.

The day after Sergo's burial, Tiniko calls Lela into her office. She offers Lela some chocolate. Lela declines. Tiniko thanks her warmly for her support at such a difficult time. She starts talking at length about something, using words like 'outlook', 'prospects' and 'aspirations'.

The school is officially responsible for the care and education of school-age children with no family. After nine years, the children are expected to leave and start new lives. In the communist era there were vocational and technical colleges and employment schemes that were legally obliged to accept these children. They were even given flats to live in. But that was then and this is now, and nowadays everyone needs a flat: refugees from Abkhazia are at the top of the list, villagers who've come to the city for a better life, large families crammed into one or two rooms; even the rich want flats, for themselves, their children, their businesses...

It's been three years since Lela finished school but she doesn't know where else to go. The staff at the school, to their credit, aren't pressuring her to leave; no one is ever forced out. There's no hope of her getting a job. After all, as Tiniko points out, if normal people can't find work, what chance is there for a girl fresh out of a school for the intellectually disabled?

Lela's the only one who's chosen to stay. Her peers have all left to make their own way in the world. Some didn't even wait to finish school. Some moved into town and started begging. One or two have found work, maybe hauling goods at the flea market or transporting produce at the market. A few have got married. Some just vanished.

Tiniko offers Lela a job watching the neighbours' cars, working out of the gatehouse. A few of the neighbours leave their cars overnight on the large forecourt in front of the school. Tiniko charges a modest monthly fee; for some, the expense is worth it if it means not coming back to missing mirrors and tyres, to a stolen radio or, worse, no car at all. Tiniko trusts Lela and thinks she will do a better job than Tariel. She'll be paid a portion of the money she collects from the neighbours and the rest will go to Tiniko for board and lodging.

Lela accepts. Tariel limps sourly out of the gatehouse, taking his few belongings with him so she can move in. With Irakli's help she brings a divan bed over from her dormitory, along with a glass from the kitchen, two sets of clothes and a handful of other items which she arranges on the small table. There's a mirror on the wall. Lela takes the cross Father Yakob gave her and attaches it to the frame.

Tariel doesn't want to give up his job. He's spent a fair few winters in the gatehouse. His wife, Narcissa, squeezed her ample hips sideways through the narrow doorway to bring him his meals every day. Once in a while Tariel's son, Gubaz, filled in for him. Thirty years old and still single, a beloved only child, Gubaz went off to do military service and promptly lost his mind. His parents sent him to hospital; the psychiatrists 'cured' him and sent him back home. Now he just wanders around in a long black coat with his hair all over the place, muttering to himself. Sometimes he makes sense, if you listen hard enough. Up and down, arguing into the wind, which carries his words away but brings no answers. The whole thing has taken its toll on Tariel and Narcissa. Their only child – who never stole, always did what he was told, excelled at maths and knew how to talk to a girl – leaves to join the army and comes back via the madhouse, transformed, tormented. Unable to bear his own reflection, he avoids mirrors. His mother took down the one on the bathroom wall so now, when Tariel wants to shave, he reaches for the shard of mirrored glass hidden under the bath, leans it against Narcissa's shampoo bottle and shaves using that, or takes his razor and bowl to the gatehouse and shaves with the mirror there.

So Tariel limps out of the school grounds, disconsolate but convinced there's no point protesting. He simply opens the gates and walks back home to where Narcissa and Gubaz are waiting for him.

Meanwhile, Lela bids farewell to the five-storey dorm block and the room she's called home for the past few years. The only reason she'll have for going into the main building now will be to use the toilet.

She goes into the gatehouse, sits on the bed and lights a cigarette. Tariel has left a large cut-glass ashtray on the table. Lela taps her ash into it. It feels strangely satisfying. Irakli comes in and sits on the bed beside her. Lela gives him the last bit of her cigarette.

Irakli is nine and has been living at the school for a year. He doesn't remember his father. It was his mother who brought him here. At first she put him in a children's home in central Georgia while she stayed in Tbilisi for work. She kept in touch, although contact was infrequent. It was hard for her to get away. Then a year ago she brought him to Tbilisi. He was to board at the school from Monday to Friday and spend the weekends with her. But the weekends passed and Irakli never did go home. When he first arrived at the school, Tiniko asked Lela to look after him. He seemed happy enough, following her around while she showed him the ropes, and Lela found him to have both quick wits and a quick tongue. As a rule, Lela felt closer to the children who were more or less 'normal'. She helped the slow kids too, when the need arose, but she kept her distance.

When Lela and Irakli go outside they see Vaska and Kolya sitting on the bench under the spruce trees.

'I'm going out,' Lela says to Kolya. 'Can you open the gates if someone needs to bring their car through?'

Kolya nods. Lela thinks she sees Vaska's smile widen, no doubt because she asked Kolya although he can't even walk properly and they both know that Vaska works the gates much better.

Lela and Irakli go round to the block of flats next door. It is almost identical to the dormitory block: a white, five-storey building with green space on all sides, some of which now houses garages. The residents here were the first to call the Residential School for Intellectually Disabled Children by its nickname, the School for Idiots. Both buildings were constructed in Khrushchev's time: one was earmarked for housing, the other was designated an auxiliary building and became the school.

They go up to the top floor and ring one of the doorbells. Mzia opens the door.

'Sorry to bother you. Do you mind if we use your phone for a minute?' asks Lela.

'Come in, come in!' says Mzia, beckoning them into the entrance hall.

The flat is spotless and smells of fresh baking. Mzia brings out a small stool for Irakli and Lela perches on the sideboard next to the telephone. They've been here before. Mzia carefully closes the doors leading off the hallway to give them some privacy.

Irakli places his index finger carefully into each hole and rotates the dial steadily. Mzia's daughter comes into the hall and stands there staring intently. Around seven or eight, she has a chubby belly, puppy-fat breasts and a large, hairy beauty spot on her cheek which reminds Lela of a furry beetle, although that's something she's never actually seen.

'Who are you phoning?' the girl asks Irakli.

'My mum,' he answers without looking up, and dials the number again.

The little girl stands in the hall for a while until she gets bored and then disappears back into the kitchen. Irakli dials again. This time he gets through.

'*Allo?*'

'Mum, it's me.'

'Irakli! How are you?' says the woman, sounding taken aback. 'I haven't managed to come home yet, Ika. I've had so much going on… I found some work but – Well, I need to look for something else. How are you, though?'

'Fine. When are you coming back?'

Irakli speaks tersely, clutching the receiver in one hand and leaning his opposite elbow on his knee.

'Next week. I already told you, remember?'

'Do you mean this week coming up?'

'Yes, don't you remember me telling you?'

Irakli hesitates.

'No, I remember,' he says. 'I thought you meant this week now, though.'

'Where are you calling from?'

'I'm at the neighbours'.'

'What's happening at your end? Are you still getting headaches?'

'No.' Silence. 'Do you remember Sergo?'

'Which Sergo?'

'From school. He died.'

'Oh, good Lord! What happened?'

'A car hit him.'

'My God, the poor thing. How awful. How did it happen?'

'He was out front in the road, walking along.'

'Oh, the poor mite…'

More silence. Lela studies Irakli's pale, pellucid skin, furrowed brow and downcast eyes.

'Are you listening to your teachers and doing what you're told?'

'Yes.'

'Good… Listen, Irakli, I've got to go. I need to get to work.'

'OK.'

'Be good. Do what your teachers tell you. And don't go out front.'

'OK.'

Lela hears the *click* as Irakli's mother puts the phone down. Irakli replaces the receiver.

'Shall we go?' says Lela, and gets to her feet.

'Yep,' says Irakli.

As they are leaving, Mzia appears and gives each of them a couple of slices of *lobiani* flat bread wrapped in newspaper so that the hot bean filling doesn't burn their fingers. They walk down the stairs in silence. Their appetites have gone.

Outside it's a warm, sunny day. Venera's son, Goderdzi, is washing his car in front of the entrance, flooding the yard with water.

'So did she say this week or next week, or can't you remember?' asks Lela, jumping over a soapy rivulet.

Irakli hops over after her.

'I dunno.'

On their way back they bump into Marika. She's only a few months older than Lela, although when they were little the age gap seemed much bigger. When they were about six, Marika used to have Lela round to play. There was one game in particular, where Marika would take Lela's knickers off, followed by her own. They'd lie down next to each other. Marika would put her hand between Lela's legs and ask Lela to do the same. Lela liked it when Marika touched her like that. She didn't like doing it back but she did it anyway, even though it left a strange scent on her hand. Marika would tell her to close her eyes and go to sleep and they'd lie there in silence, wide awake, until she decided it was time to get up again. Marika had no father and was abnormally scared of her mother.

When they got older, Marika changed the rules. One day she took Lela to the cellar and let her look between her legs. Lela saw something strange growing there. It reminded her of a cockerel's crest and the once smooth, fleshy skin surrounding it was now covered all over in thick black hair. Lela thought she'd discovered a third sex. Then Lela pulled her knickers down too and they tried to join themselves together. They stayed like that for a while, unable to quite make themselves fit. Marika warned Lela not to tell anyone what they'd done, even though they hadn't done anything wrong and the girls in her class played the same game. A few months later, when her own body started to change, Lela realized there was no third sex after all.

Then the game stopped. In fact, everything stopped. Marika stopped having Lela round and stopped coming down to the yard. Lela thought Marika must finally have realized she shouldn't be playing with retards. Now they cross paths from time to time in the yard or on the street and they always say hello. Sometimes when Lela sees Marika all grown up and walking around with her hair done nicely like other girls who have houses and parents, she wonders whether any of it really happened or whether she just made it up.

Marika is walking towards them.

'Where are you going?' Lela asks.

'I've got an English lesson,' says Marika with a warm smile.

Her auburn hair dances across her shoulders as she walks. She carries on down the road.

Lela starts eating her *lobiani*. Irakli takes a large bite out of his slice too.

'What did she actually say, then?' Lela asks.

'She says she's coming next week. She says that's what she told me last time.'

Lela brushes a scrap of newspaper off her *lobiani*, as if it's an insect, and takes a bite.

'Why do you keep sticking up for her? You know she's not coming back but you just keep ringing anyway and making an idiot of yourself.'

Irakli tears off another piece with his teeth.

'I mean, it's up to you,' says Lela. 'I wouldn't keep ringing her, though.'

They make a detour to buy cigarettes. Zaira is ill and her kiosk is closed, so they head to the kiosks further up the road.

The sun is high in the sky, bathing everything in a brilliant white light. A gentle breeze blows through the branches, caressing the leaves and sending elongated shadows dancing lazily across the tarmac. It's as if everyone has just packed up and left. Apart from an occasional car or *marshrutka* trundling down the road, kicking up clouds of dust, the street is deserted.

They stop at a dilapidated kiosk selling nothing but kerosene, matches and cigarettes. It's open, but there's no sign of the owner. A man dressed in tracksuit bottoms and flip-flops who's sitting alongside gets to his feet and wanders off into the courtyard behind the kiosk. He comes out a few moments later with a hunched but spry-looking elderly woman, presumably his mother. She goes into her tiny kiosk. Lela asks for a few cigarettes and pays.

That night a car pulls up at the gates. Lela comes out and sees Koba sitting behind the wheel of his spotlessly polished car. He winds the window down and looks at Lela standing by the gates. He seems different. Any diffidence or reserve he showed when Sergo was knocked down is gone.

He runs his eyes over Lela.

'How are you?' he asks.

'Good.'

'Where's Tariel?'

'He doesn't work here any more. It's me now.'

'Yeah? Good for you.'

Lela waits for him to drive in so that she can close the gates. He seems in no hurry.

'When can I take you for a spin, then?'

'Dunno. I'm busy.'

'Wow. You're busy *all the time*?'

Koba shakes his head and gives a forced laugh. He drives in. The yard is empty except for a scrawny dog which gives a single hoarse bark, then collapses onto the compacted earth under a spruce tree.

Lela goes back into the gatehouse. Koba parks, turns off the lights and the engine, gets out of the car and crosses over the moonlit yard towards the exit. He walks up to the gatehouse, knocks on the window, then immediately opens the door. He sees Lela sitting on the bed, smoking a cigarette.

'I'm not asking you to do it for free. I'll pay. How much do you want?'

Lela says nothing. Koba stands in the doorway in a cowboy pose, but with his scrawny frame, red palm-tree shirt and jeans, he looks more like a tourist from another Soviet republic who's ended up in Tbilisi by mistake.

'What, didn't you like it last time?' Koba asks, and smiles the strange, lopsided smile he uses to hide his rotten front teeth. Sometimes, caught off guard, he grins widely, then remembers and hurriedly shuts his lips again.

'So, what do you think? I'll take you for a spin and then bring you back. And I'll pay. I'm not expecting you to do it for free. I'm not like that.'

'No?' says Lela. 'What *are* you like?'

Koba looks slightly confused. He shifts on the spot and smiles stiffly.

'Think about it at least,' he says, and leaves.

Lela closes the door, takes a deep drag on her cigarette and exhales, watching as the smoke spreads and fades with the echoes of Koba's footsteps.

A week goes by and a few days more and there's still no sign of Irakli's mother.

Lela takes Irakli round to the flats next door. They see Goderdzi lying under his car doing some repairs while a group of young men stand around watching. Koba's there too. Rolling around on the ground, Goderdzi looks like some kind of hairy beast: his T-shirt has ridden up to his chest, revealing a stomach covered in coils of thick wavy hair growing out in all directions. Koba doesn't say hello to Lela. In fact, he pretends not to notice her at all.

Mzia opens the door. She's still smiling. A pleasant spring breeze rushes through the open windows and makes the curtain on the back of the door flutter wildly.

They sit as before: Irakli on the stool and Lela on the sideboard.

Irakli dials. The phone on the other end rings, but nobody picks up, so Irakli calls a neighbour instead. A man answers.

'Can I speak to Inga, please?' asks Irakli.

There's a long silence, then a woman comes on the line. It doesn't sound like Irakli's mother.

'Who is this?'

'It's Irakli, Inga's son...'

'Oh, hello, Irakli. How are you, love? It's Nana Ivlita – remember me?'

'Yes.'

'Your mum's not here, Irakli. She's in Greece. She said to tell you she'll be back, though. She's going to take you to live with her over there.'

The woman is shouting so loud Lela thinks she must have forgotten she's got the phone there at all and is trying to make herself heard without it.

For a moment Irakli says nothing.

'When's she coming back?'

'She said she doesn't know yet. She needs to find a job first, you see. Anyway, how are you, dear?'

'Fine.'

Irakli sits there, hunched over, one hand holding the receiver, the other braced against his knee. Lela looks at his downcast eyes and – for the millionth time – is struck by the way his long eyelashes curve up at the end.

'What shall I tell Inga when she calls, love? Do you want me to give her a message?'

Irakli thinks for a moment.

'Ask her when she's coming back.'

'OK. I'll do that.'

'OK.'

'Take care, Irakli, and try not to worry. Bye-bye.'

Irakli puts the phone down.

'Ready?' says Lela.

'Ready.'

As they are leaving, Mzia smiles at them and slips a couple of barberry sweets into their pockets.

They walk along in silence until Irakli suddenly asks, 'Do you think she's actually gone?'

Lela unwraps one of her barberry sweets.

'Probably,' she says, pulling the sticky sweet out of the wrapper with her teeth. She offers the other one to Irakli. 'Try one. They're really nice.'

'I've got my own,' he says.

They carry on walking. Irakli stares down at the ground. His pale ears look like diaphanous red-ribbed leaves against the glow of the setting sun.

3

There are no 'Heroes of Kerch Street'. At least not yet.
It took thirty-one years for the city of Kerch to receive
its title. Maybe one day a child from this foul-smelling,
crumbling school will be given the title as well. If that day
ever comes, there's no doubt who the school's first heroes
will be: Kirile and Ira.

They left a few years back – Kirile first, Ira five years
later – and the more time passes, the harder it is to believe
that such gifted, successful people ever lived there. Lela and
the others have heard all about them from the teachers.

Kirile didn't break his ties with the school straight
away. Lela was still young when he left but she remembers
him visiting. He was tall and slim, a slouching, fair-haired
Russian boy with a calm voice and an unhurried gait. He
wore flared trousers and from a distance he reminded Lela
of one of the Bremen Town Musicians from the old Soviet
cartoon. She couldn't get the image out of her mind: Kirile
walking down the road, hunched over, arms swinging,
holding a bag in one hand. He looked like a tired old man
coming home from work. The children would run out to
meet him whether they knew him or not. Kirile would

smile, say hello, pull sweets out of his bag and hand them round. Dali would look on with tears in her eyes, brimming with pride to see what a fine, upstanding man he had become. What set Kirile apart was that he graduated from school with distinction, went on to university and then found a job. Although he lived at the school, he was such a capable student that they sent him to a 'normal' school, where his exam results earned him a gold medal. When Kirile visited, he never stayed for more than an hour. He had the weary, sad expression of a man carrying a heavy weight on his shoulders. It was clear that his life was filled with worry and woe.

Then, like so many others, Kirile disappeared without a trace. Some said he'd gone to Russia, others that he'd been killed. Nobody knew for sure. Slowly but surely the myth of Kirile was forgotten; soon even Dali stopped mentioning him.

The second hero would no doubt be Ira, a blonde girl with a Georgian father and a Russian mother. Her father left her mother and her mother left her children in turn. Ira could tell you off the top of her head which residential school or children's home each of her many brothers and sisters was in. She was charming and elegant, the kind of girl who could wander into the yard next door without anyone suspecting she was connected with the School for Idiots. Like Kirile, she graduated from school with distinction and later went on to university to study law. Ira's heroism went one step further, though. She took her own mother to court to strip her of her parental rights and, miraculously, she won. She took custody of her youngest sibling, who for some reason the mother had chosen to keep, and raised him herself. Dali loved Ira's story. Whenever she thought about it her eyes filled with tears.

Lela remembers Ira well. Eventually Ira got married and cut her hair short, but she still came back for the occasional visit. She was as happy and charming as ever. She would run straight over to the playground to play football with the children, making deft tackles and then racing off towards the goal in her short leather skirt and crop top, laughing loudly, without a care in the world.

So far, Kirile and Ira are the only future heroes the school has produced. The children always found their stories fascinating. If Kirile and Ira were backward like them, they asked, how had they managed to finish school? How had they managed to *learn*? The teachers told them that some of the children at the school – like Kolya and Stella – were not actually backward at all but were living here because the children's homes were full or because of the school's superior facilities, like its big yard and playground, and the quality of its teaching staff.

There are others, though, who might never be considered heroes but who nonetheless stand out in the history of the school.

Lela remembers Marcel, a fifteen-year-old black boy from Batumi, a wild, unbroken colt with a fiery temper. Nobody seemed to know how he ended up in Tbilisi. To the locals, who had never seen a black person before except on TV, Marcel was like a museum exhibit. They would come from all over Gldani to stare at him through the school fence, shouting, 'Hey, darkie, come over here!' Marcel would bend down, pick up gravel by the handful and throw it at them, or press himself against the fence like a caged animal, clawing, howling and spitting.

Marcel intrigued Lela. He paid no attention to the teachers and did whatever he wanted. He spoke to Lela on just three occasions, but each time he was calm and articulate.

The first time, Marcel came up to her in the dinner hall and asked whether the cooks put dead flies in the food. The second time, they were in the yard and he asked about bus routes. The third time was at night. Lela couldn't sleep so she went down to the yard for a cigarette. She didn't notice him at first in the darkness. Then he whistled and she spotted him sitting on the bench under the spruces. He waved at her to come over, then asked for a cigarette.

She sat down on the bench next to him. They smoked in silence. Marcel took long, deep drags. When he had finished, Lela offered him another cigarette. He took it, stood up and walked away, then turned to call back to Lela: 'Is the sea near here?'

She replied, 'No.'

He turned again and left, and that was the end of that.

A few days later they took Marcel away. Lela never knew where he was taken or why.

There was Aksana, a pretty, smiling girl with blonde hair and blue eyes who, unlike the other girls at the school, refused to dress like a tomboy. Instead, she wore tight skirts and light dresses. She was constantly disappearing with young men from the neighbourhood and coming back with pockets full of sweets and trinkets. If Aksana's name was mentioned by anyone outside the school, it was usually because she had 'fucked half of Gldani' or gone at someone's dick 'like it was a Chupa Chups lollipop'. She was always smiling, though. Lela only once saw her cry. Lela was riding Marika's bike up and down when she saw Aksana coming out of the yard behind the College of Light Industry down the road from the school. She was crying. When Lela asked who'd upset her, Aksana just started sobbing more violently and repeating, 'The bastard, the bastard.' Lela gave her a ride back to the school on Marika's bike and by the time she got off and blended back into the crowd of schoolchildren the smile had returned to her face.

Then one day Aksana left, with no warning, not even a goodbye, joining the ranks of so many others before her who vanished as if they had never existed.

Then there was Ilona, a wilful, free-spirited Lom gypsy girl who answered to no one. When a journalist visited the school, Ilona told her that Vano had fucked her. Tiniko ignored her but the journalist spent some time going around the school trying to investigate what had happened and, as Tiniko had no objections, filming the children. Lela remembers Tiniko telling the journalist about Aksana, who wasn't the only girl from the school to have gone down that path. They just couldn't stop her, Tiniko explained: once she'd gone out they had no idea *what* she was up to; they weren't children any more, they were *adults*; it was just *in their nature*; they wanted it too, especially if there were sweets and presents on offer. The journalist listened carefully. She spoke to the children, asked them questions, wrote down their answers and made pages of notes. Then, for some reason, she too just disappeared, taking what Tiniko and Ilona had said with her.

Ilona left and started begging and selling herself at the station, or so the children were told. They heard she'd moved back to her parents' on Lotkin Street. They heard that one day her parents got into a fight, that Ilona's mother and little brother hid in the wardrobe and her father fetched his gun and emptied the entire clip through the wardrobe door, into his son. After the incident Ilona's father took her to Russia and that was the last that was heard of her.

There was another girl, called Yana. Lela remembers her well; they were the same age. Yana was proud and self-assured. She talked non-stop about her parents and her grandmother, all of whom were dead, but most of all about her uncle, her only living relative, who, she was certain, would take care of her once she left school. According to Yana, her parents' flat was waiting for her, all sealed up and held as part of their estate until she turned eighteen. She was one of those people who came out of any situation looking good. She didn't fight, she didn't swear and she never complained or took offence, although she never looked particularly happy either.

One day Yana asked Lela to come to the flats next door. It was New Year's Day and bitterly cold outside; the children were all huddled indoors. The streets were empty apart from a few hungry dogs. Yana took Lela into the yard, then rolled up her sleeves and started digging around in the bins. Lela did the same. At that moment a woman opened a window on the third floor and beckoned to them. Yana and Lela went over to the foot of the building. The woman disappeared inside and two little girls stuck their heads out and shouted down to Yana and Lela to wait. The woman reappeared, balanced a basket on the window ledge and tied a rope to the handle. Then she began to lower it carefully out of the window. Lela and Yana stood there, hearts pounding, waiting for it to reach them. The closer it came, the more they could see: the basket had been filled to the brim with sweets, cakes, dried fruit, walnut *churchkhela* and mandarin oranges.

'Take it! It's for you!' shouted one of the girls.

Yana took the basket and untied the rope, and the two of them raced back to the school as fast as they could.

When Lela and Yana ran in carrying the basket the other children could hardly believe their eyes. In no time at all there was nothing left but the mandarin skins. Lela can still recall how good the cake tasted. Years later, when chocolate imported from Turkey started appearing in the kiosks, she would sometimes buy a Mars or a Snickers but always found herself thinking that nothing would ever taste better than that cake.

Less than an hour later, Yana told Lela they were going back to return the basket.

Yana emerged from the TV room with a few of the other children. Lela couldn't work out how Yana had chosen them; most of them had trouble either walking or speaking. Yana led Lela and the other five children round to the block next door.

The little girl who opened the door looked quite startled when she saw such a large group of children. Then the woman came to the door and invited the children inside.

It was the first time in Lela's life that she had been invited to a *supra*. The table was out in the loggia. The woman laid it with crockery, cutlery and even serviettes, then brought out more food than Lela had ever seen: fried chicken, walnut sauce, cheese-filled *khachapuri*, stuffed vine leaves, cake, caramelized walnut *gozinaqi*, bread, dried fruit, fizzy drinks and stewed quinces.

The children sat down to eat. The television in the corner was showing a New Year's concert and while the children tucked in the woman asked them questions about how they had seen in the New Year. She wanted to know whether the school had welcomed its first visitor of the year yet and then told them that Yana herself had been the first person to come to their door. So full she could hardly breathe, Yana laughed to think of her honoured role. The woman's daughters asked whether there was a New Year tree at the school. The girls had an artificial tree in the corner of the loggia and had covered the floor and branches with cotton wool as imitation snow. The youngest girl pressed a button at the base of the tree, which began to rotate slowly. The children clapped and stared, mesmerized, at the toys and ornaments hanging from the branches, finding their reflections in the succession of shiny baubles that passed in front of them as the tree turned.

When they had finished, the woman packed the leftovers into the empty basket and sent it home with the children.

That was Yana, the girl who could go out to look through bins and come back with a basket of goodies – twice.

Some time later Yana became ill. Nobody knew what was wrong with her. One day an ambulance came and took her away, pale, weak and unable to eat or speak. Then they got word that Yana had moved in with her uncle and would not be coming back.

Like Lela, Yana would be eighteen now. Lela wonders whether Yana is living in her parents' flat now, and whether she still buttons her shirt right up to the neck. Or whether she is even alive.

One by one, all of the pupils that Lela remembers have left the school. Times have changed. The children who used to live there seemed more rebellious, readier to fight and run away. Nowadays things are much calmer. New children hardly ever join the school and Lela is the only former pupil still living there.

As such, she occupies the most powerful position in the school. Nobody tells her what to do and nobody messes her around. When Lela was a little girl hiding in the teachers' skirts, she could never have imagined a time would come when she was scared of nobody. Yet because there is nobody left to be frightened of, life seems to have lost its edge and time itself seems sluggish.

The departure of certain children saw the end of a brutal tradition, a 'game' Lela was never made to play. Merely witnessing it had terrified her. Lela saw it first-hand in Marcel's time. The older children would grab a new girl or a girl in her early teens, drag her off to the pear field and deliver her to some libidinous boy, who would push her onto the ground and then rape her, while the others, both boys and girls, held her down by the arms and legs. The sound of the girl's cries made Lela's heart beat out of her chest. The children would clamp their hands over the girl's mouth to silence the screams. The sight of the girl lying there filled Lela with horror: the splayed legs, the scratches on her face, the blood... When the boy had finished he would get up and the children would drift back to the playground to carry on with their games, leaving the girl lying there on the ground. Then she would stand up too, straighten her clothes and spend a few minutes by herself before rejoining the others and carrying on as normal. The victims of this game were usually girls who wore skirts and dresses and grew their hair long.

After the collapse of the Soviet Union everything in the school began to break down, starting with the taps and ending with the balcony. The school started receiving humanitarian aid and second-hand clothes, which had never happened before, but only rarely did any of it reach the children. Tiniko 'redirected' most of the items to line her own pockets, if the official in charge of dividing the goods between the schools had not already done so.

The school began to lose teachers as well. Only Tiniko, Dali, Vano and Gulnara are left from the old guard. Nowadays new teachers come, they teach a few lessons, realize the school has nothing to offer them and go again. New children have stopped arriving too. Maybe parents today are less willing to abandon their children or maybe there are better schools out there to abandon them in. Maybe idiots just aren't being born any more.

That is why everyone is so surprised when one day the gates open and a well-dressed young woman in her thirties walks in with a girl aged about nine. The girl looks smart and well cared for but also nervous and guarded. Lela strokes the little girl's hair, then walks them over to Tiniko's office. Tiniko is expecting them. The woman explains that the little girl is related to her husband. Having lost her parents, she was being raised by her grandmother. Now that she too has died, the child's relatives have decided to leave her with the school.

Tiniko shows them around with a large group of children in tow.

'Do you like it here, Nona?' the woman asks with a forced smile, looking down at the little girl. 'Look what a big yard they have!'

'The baths and showers are in here,' says Tiniko, 'and this is also where they do the laundry. The whole site belongs to us. The children spend plenty of time outside in the fresh air. Over there we have the dinner hall...'

'You won't be bored, will you? Look at all the nice children!'

The woman turns around to the children and gives them an exaggerated look of surprise, as if seeing them properly for the first time.

'Oh, look! They're so sweet!' She goes up to Stella, who's standing in the front row, cups her cheek and asks, 'What's your name?'

'Stella!' she answers happily.

'Oh, you're just delightful!' says the woman, and strokes Stella's cheek. Stella blushes shyly and gives a broad smile.

Lela can't understand why the woman is planning to leave this pretty and apparently well-loved girl at the school.

'We'll come to see you every weekend. If we can't come to you, you can come to us,' the lady says, hugging Nona.

The girl looks embarrassed and wraps her arms around the woman hesitantly, as if she hasn't known her for very long.

For the next few days Irakli is out of sorts. Nona, he realizes, is competition. Lela takes Nona under her wing. She moves one of the little ones to a different part of the girl's dormitory and puts Nona's bed in the prime spot by the windows. The other children are eager to see what Nona has in her little suitcase. She lets the other children look, while Lela keeps a watchful eye to make sure nobody takes anything. Stella is totally smitten with Nona, who gives her one of her dresses. From that moment on, Stella doesn't run around dressed only in leggings; now she wears leggings and a pink, frilly jersey dress too.

*

It's the afternoon. The children have had their lunch. Vano's in charge today, which means everything should run smoothly.

It's a bright, windy day and the children are playing football. A few of the children from next door have come to join in, which raises the stakes considerably. Irakli is fired up and playing so hard that he's sweating heavily. Even the normally quiet Kolya is a completely different person when he's playing football. He starts shouting and waving his arms around and, if a child from the school scores against the 'normal' kids, he throws himself on the ground and roars with happiness.

The match ends in victory for the 'normal' kids. The children disperse. Lela, who was refereeing, notices that Nona has gone.

'Irakli,' she says, 'have you seen Nona?'

'No,' he replies, and runs off towards the drinking fountain.

'Vano called her inside,' says one of the others.

Lela heads quickly over to the school building and sees Vano coming out with Nona behind him. Vano is holding the class register and what looks like a textbook. Nona is holding a book too, clutching it to her chest.

'You can keep that. Now go and play,' Vano tells her, and walks down the steps. Nona just stands there looking dazed and disoriented, as if she doesn't know where to go next.

Lela stares at Nona and sees she's been crying. There are lines on her face where the tears have run down her grubby cheeks. Lela stops dead in her tracks, choked with rage, throat burning, heart pounding, and stares at Vano, who is already halfway across the yard on his way to the drinking fountain.

Lela stands rooted to the spot. Nona is still at the top of the steps, still clutching the book to her chest, still wearing the dress she had on when she arrived, although now it is ripped and dirty. Her once neatly plaited hair hangs loose and dishevelled.

'There you go,' Vaska says, walking up behind Lela. 'The new kid's right there.'

He sits down by the drinking fountain where Vano is still standing, thirstily gulping down water.

Nona starts walking gingerly down the steps. Lela stares at her, trying to interpret her expression, trying to place that look on her face. Nona doesn't look much different from how she did before, except that now, like her dress, she seems damaged, soiled, tear-stained... Vano stops drinking and walks off.

Vaska watches him go, then sits down on the pavement. He wipes the sweat off his face with the hem of his T-shirt and shouts over to Nona, 'Quick shag, was it?' He laughs.

Nona doesn't understand and carries on down the steps.

Without even thinking, Lela runs at Vaska, who is still sitting on the pavement, and kicks him hard in the face. Caught off guard, Vaska falls back onto the pavement. Lela kicks him again and again and Vaska can do nothing to defend himself.

The other children start running over from all directions. One shouts out in a panic, 'She's beating up Vaska! She's beating up Vaska!'

Vaska struggles onto all fours and manages to get to his feet.

'You bastard, what did you say?' screams Lela, and punches Vaska in the chest. 'What did you say, you little shit? Say it again!'

Vaska has blood pouring from his nose.

'Nothing! What's wrong with you?'

'What's wrong? I'll fucking show you what's wrong. Now tell me what you said!'

Vaska tries to get away.

'What did he say? What did he say?' ask the others.

Once again Lela launches herself at Vaska, who thinks it's all over and is already wiping the blood from his nose with his T-shirt. A few of the children try to hold Lela back. She feels someone grab hold of her arm. Irakli, who only comes up to her shoulders, looks her straight in the eye and shouts, 'Lela, stop it, now!'

She looks at Irakli in astonishment, although she doesn't really know why. She stops and lets out a deep sigh. Vaska goes over to the drinking fountain and washes the blood off his face. The other children go with him, leaving Lela and Irakli standing there, alone.

A week later a relative from the village comes for Nona. She's only a young woman but her face is deeply lined and weathered. Nona doesn't know the woman but goes with her anyway. The woman shows Tiniko some documents, signs a few pieces of paper and takes Nona, her dirty dress and her little suitcase away from the school for ever.

Lela lets them out through the gates. Stella sits on the bench under the spruce trees and cries.

4

Lela dreams she's taking Sergo round to use the phone,
not Irakli. Sergo's got Tiniko's pink dress tucked under
his arm. They walk up the stairs and Lela asks him who
the hell he's phoning anyway, given that he has no mother,
given that he hasn't got anyone. Sergo says nothing. He
walks up to the door and rings the bell.

Mzia invites them in. She doesn't seem at all surprised
to see Lela with Sergo instead of Irakli. She leaves them
in the hallway. Sergo lifts the receiver and dials, but it's
not a local number. Instead of six digits, this one has
seven, eight, nine, more. The dial patiently clicks round
and the number seems never to end... Lela asks where
it is he's calling, but Sergo doesn't reply, just dials and
dials. Mzia's daughter lies there in a ball on the floor,
screwed up like a discarded cleaning cloth. Everyone's
pretending she's not there. She moans softly, peeking out
miserably like a poorly child from her sickbed. Lela notices
that the girl's beetle beauty spot has grown and spread
to cover half her face. Suddenly Piruz, the local police
inspector, emerges from the other room, deep in thought,
with Mzia behind him. He walks over to the front door

looking tired and troubled. Mzia opens the door. Piruz hesitates, then shrugs.

'We don't have that kind of thing here. Have they lost their minds?' he says, and leaves.

Mzia closes the door and that's when Lela notices the blood pouring out of a huge gash in the back of her head. Lela is terrified but doesn't wake up, and suddenly she's outside in the street with Sergo, and Irakli's there too. They're late; they hurry along and as they near the gates they see a crowd of locals and schoolchildren. There's a bus at the side of the road. People are waiting. It looks like a funeral. Then Vano and Tiniko come through the gates. Tiniko is clutching Vano's arm. She looks weak and unwell, barely able to drag her legs along. She moans softly and the hot summer breeze carries the sound to the sombre, now silent crowd. Lela suddenly realizes this is Tiniko's funeral. She's wearing that same pink dress Sergo had under his arm. The right side is covered in blood. Zaira's there too, and Avto and Levan, and Vaska with that stupid smile. Levan comes over.

'Tiniko's been fucked so hard she can hardly walk!'

He laughs.

'Go to hell,' says Irakli.

It's time to leave for the cemetery. Vano and Tiniko carry on towards the bus, slowly, like pallbearers carrying a coffin.

Zaira comes up to Tiniko.

'And to think you said that dress didn't suit you!' she says cheerfully.

Tiniko doesn't answer. She steps up onto the bus looking mournful.

The bus moves off. Lela spots Aksana standing in the rear window, smiling at her. She feels someone touch her on the shoulder. She turns around and sees Tiniko. Startled, she tries to tell her that she should be on the bus but the words stick in her throat, choking her. Tiniko starts squeezing her arm harder. 'You see? Now we're in trouble… And if the Board decides to inspect us…' Tiniko tightens her grip and won't let go, and Lela tries to shout, 'Get off me!' but the sound won't leave her throat… She forces the words out in a hoarse rasp, followed by a feral roar which jolts her from her sleep.

She stands up, sweat-soaked, feels around for the bulb on the low ceiling and gives it a twist. She hears the metallic grind of the screw-thread and a flickering yellow light floods the gatehouse.

Lela sits on the bed for a few minutes. She's wearing just a T-shirt and knickers. She pushes her fingers through her hair and takes a deep breath. The dream flashes through her mind. She can still feel the fear. She pulls on her trousers, feels around with her feet for her shoes and goes outside.

Lela sits on the bench under the spruce trees. She smokes a cigarette, gradually composing herself, and wonders whether a dream like that means she really is mad. She stares down at the bench, a plank wedged at each end into a deep slit sawn in a tree trunk. It's the only bench in the yard and it's been here for as long as anyone can remember. Both trees are living, growing, desperately trying to hold their half-sawn trunks together so that the soil's nutrients can reach their upper branches; the plank anchors and links these two spruces, taken captive by man, held captive by each other, destined to live for evermore with a foreign body fused into their trunks.

Lela gets to her feet and starts pacing. The moon is shining daylight-bright in the yard. The school buildings are shrouded in darkness. There's total silence; a few cars on the forecourt; the old Lada that's been there for years, with no owner and no one to tow it away, abandoned, caked in bird droppings, falling apart. Lela stares at it for a while, until her attention is caught by headlights approaching fast down the road. She thinks of Sergo. In the distance she hears the light *pat-pat-pat* of a dog walking across asphalt and the sound a man makes heading home late at night.

Lela throws the butt away and goes back to her room. She unhooks a T-shirt from a nail on the wall, waves aside a cloud of gnats and carefully unscrews the red-hot bulb. Darkness envelops her. She lies down. Bit by bit her surroundings emerge and take shape: the door, window and table, the spruce branch outside, swaying in the breeze, and the shadow it casts, swaying in time. She drifts off into sleep.

Lela wakes the next morning to the sound of a child's loud cries. Disoriented, she gets up, throws on some clothes and goes outside. The sun is already high in the sky. It must have rained in the night; the morning air feels pleasantly cold against her skin. There's a large group of children standing by the gates, peering out to see who's crying. Lela hurries over, shoves them to one side and sees a young woman standing just outside with a boy of around five, who is clutching her hand and sobbing loudly.

'Shall I leave you here? Is that what you want?' the woman asks him, yanking her hand around to try and shake him off.

'Nooooo,' wails the boy, clinging to his mother as best he can. He has large dark eyes and short, spiky hair. They live in the block next door and this isn't the first time she's brought her son up to the gates like this.

'Have a good look! These children didn't do what they were told either so their mummies and daddies brought them here!' she says, pointing at the children peering wide-eyed through the gates at them.

'Well? Are you going to do it again?'

'No,' he says tearfully.

'Don't be scared! We won't eat you!' Levan shouts.

The children laugh. Lela notices Vaska standing near Levan. His face is covered in purple bruises and he has a large black eye.

The little boy bursts into tears.

'Well then? Shall I leave you here or take you home?' She turns towards the children and shouts theatrically through the fence, 'Children, where's your teacher? I've got a new child for you!'

The boy cries even more loudly and clings to his mother's legs. Trying not to laugh, the woman pats him affectionately.

'There, there, it's OK. I won't leave you here this time. But only if you do what you're told.'

'I will,' the boy says, his voice trembling.

They set off home.

*

The children disperse, most running over to the dinner hall, where Goderdzi will be holding his wedding reception the following day. Neighbourhood weddings and wakes are often held in the school. After all, who has room at home to host, feed and water five hundred guests? The children have all been invited and are over the moon; it's rare for them to get the chance to play host.

The women from the flats next door are busy in the kitchens. They are not particularly close to Venera or Goderdzi but it's tradition that when someone in the building dies the neighbours organize the wake and when someone gets married they organize the reception.

The women are making whatever they can in advance. They'll prepare the hot food tomorrow. There's a steady back-and-forth between the neighbouring flats and the school, but via the adjoining courtyards rather than through the main gates. Avto has widened the gap in the fence so that the women can squeeze through with their dishes and bowls without catching their clothes on the wire. They make their way across the playground and down the path alongside the pear field before coming out by the dinner hall, where they find a large group of children milling around, desperate to be given jobs to do.

Lela is in the dinner hall, lifting the large pots down from the shelves. Meanwhile, Koba and the other boys are bringing in boxes of rented crockery. Irakli walks ahead, clearing a path.

'Hey, Lela,' says Irakli. 'Can you come outside for a sec?'

Lela hurries after him along the path that borders the pear field.

'Hurry up!' he says, and points up the path at Mzia, who's popping home to fetch her walnut-grinder.

'Mzia's going home to get something,' he says, racing ahead. 'She might let us use the phone…'

'Are you soft in the head?' Lela snaps. 'You can't call her, can you, because she's gone to Greece, you idiot.'

'I'm gonna ring Ivlita. She might have a number for Mum. And if not… well, then I won't call.'

Irakli navigates the gap in the fence. He looks back to see Lela still standing in the school grounds staring at him.

'What do you need me for, then? Go and ring her!'

She turns and starts heading back.

'Lela, please!' Irakli calls.

She turns back and looks at Irakli through the gap in the fence. In the distance she sees Mzia striding up into the tower block.

'Just one more time, Lela. I'll never ask you again, I swear!'

Lela looks at Irakli's big ears and ardent expression and can't help but laugh.

'You'd better not,' she says, and steps through the fence.

They find Mzia on the landing. She shows them inside, brings out the small stool and disappears into the kitchen.

Irakli calls Ivlita and asks for a number for his mother in Greece. Lela asks Mzia for a pen and paper, then writes down the number as Irakli reads it out.

Irakli says goodbye, hangs up and stares at the piece of paper for a while.

'Read it for me,' he says with determination.

Lela reads out the number.

Irakli dials. The phone on the other end rings, then Lela hears a familiar voice.

'Mum, it's me,' says Irakli weakly.

'Irakli!' she says, sounding pleased but surprised. 'How are you? I still haven't made it home, have I? Things have been so crazy... I've been so busy, so much to do... and I didn't have the money to come... But I'm about to start work and then I'll have enough to come home. I should send you some presents, shouldn't I...'

'When are you coming home?' asks Irakli.

'I've just started a new job. I need to save up a bit and then I'll come back...'

Silence.

'Irakli, you know I love you, right? Don't be cross. It's better this way...'

Irakli's eyes fill with tears. He rubs his eyes vigorously to try and stem the flow. He goes bright red and screws up his face, but no sound comes out. He just sits there in silence on the stool.

Lela snatches the phone out of his hand and shouts into the receiver, 'It's better this way, is it? You bitch, dumping your kid and swanning off like that! What kind of a mother are you? You fucking waste of space! Stop promising him you'll come back! Stop promising things, you miserable cow!'

Irakli stares at Lela in disbelief. Lela is leaning forward, receiver in one hand, the other hand braced against her knee, sitting just like Irakli does.

A voice comes from the receiver: 'Hello? Hello? Who is this?'

'None of your fucking business! Listen, either you stop lying to him or I will come to Greece and I'll fucking well stop you myself!'

She slams the receiver down.

'Come on, we're going. Hurry up!' she says, as if she's expecting Irakli's mother to come after them. 'Thank you!' Lela calls out as they leave.

They go back in silence. Irakli is crying.

'What are you crying for, you big baby?' Lela says, walking faster. 'Don't you get it? She's not coming. She just can't bring herself to tell you! I told you she wasn't coming and you wouldn't listen! What do you need a mother for anyway? You know how to walk and talk, how to eat! You're all grown up, for God's sake!'

The minute they walk into the yard all thoughts of Irakli's mother are forgotten. The school has a visitor: a woman called Madonna, who is taking photos of the children with a small silver camera. Dali is shouting instructions: 'Stand up straight! Smile!' Lela notices that Madonna is only photographing three children: Pako, a girl called Jilda and a boy called Lasha. All three are about six years old and have been scrubbed and dressed smartly. The children take turns to stand against the wall Madonna has chosen as a backdrop.

Madonna has bleach-blonde hair and an unusually ample rear end which she hauls around like a foreign body. Pako stands against the wall, hair wet-combed to one side, and when Dali tells him to stand up straight he pulls himself up so tall Lela thinks he might snap in the middle. Lasha is next. He stands by the wall with his big, sad eyes. Dali goes to straighten his hair and shirt. Madonna tries to get his attention, clicking her fingers above her head. Lasha just looks bewildered.

'Will you please just *smile*, boy?' Dali says crossly.

Lasha attempts a smile and bares his teeth, but with his brow still furrowed he looks even more wretched. The other children start laughing.

'Christ, who'd pick him? I mean, look at him!' Levan says gleefully.

'Uffff,' sighs Tiniko suddenly. 'We had such a nice little girl – Nona. Her family took her back, though. She was so much better than this lot – one look at her and they'd have snapped her up, I tell you. She was so pretty, so bright…'

'You're right,' says Dali sadly. 'We don't get kids like Nona every day.'

It's Jilda's turn, but Tiniko's not convinced. Jilda is seven, a slight girl with straight black hair and a squint in one eye, and is a Yazidi, which in Tiniko's opinion makes her an unsuitable candidate for international adoption.

Madonna sits down for a quick rest. She lights a cigarette and fiddles with her camera. The whole school is there watching the three children closely.

Madonna, it transpires, has spent several years working for an American couple as a carer and is now helping them find a child to adopt. The compassion and self-sacrifice she demonstrated while caring for the wife's elderly mother led the couple to develop a deep respect for her country, Georgia. Having cared for and lost a disabled child themselves, they decided to adopt from a residential school, so Madonna is visiting schools in Tbilisi to take photos of children aged around six. There are other children that age in the school, but Tiniko has chosen the three she considers the most attractive and whose parents – significantly – have formally relinquished responsibility, leaving the children's fate entirely in the hands of the school and the Ministry.

'You'll need to write their full names down for me and a bit of background,' says Madonna. 'They want some idea about who they're bringing into their family.'

'Aren't you taking pictures of the others?' Lela says, coming towards them.

Before Tiniko can answer, Levan sticks his head out of the crowd and scoffs, 'They want the little ones, don't they, not big lugs like us!'

'Oh, Levan, if only your wit had a chance to sparkle somewhere else for a change,' says Tiniko pityingly, only too aware that nobody will be coming to save him from the hardships of life in Georgia.

Madonna says she would like photos of the children playing. Pako wants them to be playing football but the ball's half deflated. Jilda runs off to do some skipping, but Pako and Lasha just stand there stiffly. Their neatly combed hair and scrubbed faces seem to be putting them off their game.

'Fine, never mind. Hopscotch, then. Pretend you're playing hopscotch.'

Tiniko feels someone's hand on her elbow. She turns around to find Lela standing there.

'Tiniko, I really need to talk to you.'

She eyes Lela suspiciously, asks Madonna to excuse her and takes her to one side.

'Well?'

'Tiniko,' says Lela, 'can you ask her to take pictures of the others too? The little ones, I mean.'

Tiniko sighs. She whispers, 'OK, tell me which ones. You know I value your opinion.'

'Well... all of them. Just the little ones, I mean. But tell her not to just take the photos. She needs to show them to the Americans too. You never know, they might like Stella. Or even Levan.'

'No, no. Even if they do like Levan they can't have him. His mum's still around, so we wouldn't be allowed to send him. But all right, let's do Stella, and some of the others...' They go back to Madonna and Tiniko lowers her voice. 'It's the paperwork, you see. If they've still got parents I can't send them anywhere. I don't want to end up in prison. We'll do the kids who've got no family.'

The other children are neither dressed smartly nor particularly clean, but they line up against the wall and do what Dali and Madonna tell them. Madonna takes photos of practically every child under ten who has no family or whose relatives have given them up. Stella wets her hands in the drinking fountain, tries to flatten her hair, runs over to the wall and stands stock-still, a smile on her face, waiting for her photo.

'Where's Irakli?' asks Tiniko, looking around.

Lela thinks she must have misheard. But no, it appears that Irakli's mother has chosen Greece over her son and given him up for good. Lela steels herself and walks back to the school, determined to find Irakli and tell him the truth. She wishes she'd said even worse things to his mother. All she can think now is that Irakli needs to know. He needs to know that his bitch of a mother abandoned him and that he had *no fucking idea*.

She finds Irakli by himself, lying on a bed. He's not crying. He's just lying on his back and hiding his face with his arm. As soon as Lela sees him she changes her mind.

'Come on, Tiniko's looking for you. You need to have your photo taken. You might even get lucky.'

'I don't want to.'

Lela pulls Irakli's arm away from his face and tickles him. 'Come on, it'll be fun. They won't really send you to America. They want someone little and cute, not some big lump like you! Come on, shift your bum!'

Irakli says nothing.

'Are you upset cos I swore at your mum?'

Irakli closes his eyes and presses himself even harder against the wall.

'You're scared she'll be angry and won't come back, right?' Lela thinks for a minute. 'You don't need to worry.

We'll give her a ring and you can tell her it was just some psycho who grabbed the phone... Someone who's not quite right in the head. One of the others. Tell her they swear at everyone like that.'

Irakli starts to cry.

'Ika, come on. We'll call her back and you can tell her someone grabbed the phone off you! Tell her they got thrown out of school, or even better, tell her they're dead! Tell her they got hit by a car!'

Lela tries to roll Irakli over towards her.

'Come on, don't be a baby. She had it coming. She was lying to you! Stop being silly!'

Lela grabs Irakli by the arm and yanks him across the bed.

'What do you want from me? I'll take you over tomorrow!' she says angrily, shaking him by the arms. 'I'll take you right now if you want, but tell her it was some random mad person cos I'm not going to apologize, OK? And if she doesn't believe you she can fuck right off!'

Lela grabs Irakli by the wrist and drags him into the corridor.

They go back down to the yard. Lela drags Irakli over to the wall, shunts the line of children to one side and shoves Irakli in, right in front of Madonna's camera.

'Who's gonna want him!' titters Levan. 'Who's gonna want him in their house with those head lice! You've got lice, right, Ika?'

Lela rewards Levan with a crack on the back of the head.

*

It's the day of the wedding. Mzia and one of her neighbours are holding a large red velvet sheet against the wall while Avto bangs nails into the corners. The woman who years ago had lowered that New Year's feast down to the children starts pinning bunches of tiny white roses to the velvet.

A long table is set up in front of the velvet and laid with decorated porcelain and fancy glasses. The children's table is set up in the second, smaller hall, which runs the length of the main hall.

One of the women waddles out of the kitchen and, looking up and down the children's table, asks, 'Should we give them the whole works too?'

The organizer, a gaunt woman with a stern, pock-marked face, nods to the cook.

'Even the wine?' she asks.

The woman hesitates, then looks over at Avto.

'A glass each won't kill them,' he says, 'and then they can join in with the toasts. Put some soft drinks out too. You know what kids like.'

Lela hears the long celebratory blast of car horns. She opens the gates to let the cars drive in, shuts them again and walks in behind the cars. Dali shepherds the children away. She is already in her wedding outfit: a black blouse with green polka dots and green lace around the neckline. Goderdzi gets out of the bridal car wearing a suit and looking as clean as a whistle. He walks round to the other side for his bride, Manana. She steps out, a vision of unparalleled beauty in a long white dress, with long, plaited black hair and a wide, captivating smile. The neighbours look her up and down in astonishment, transfixed by her slow, elegant gait and the way her dress strains against her body as she breathes.

'Looks like she's done quite a bit of entertaining already,' Lela hears one of the neighbours whisper. 'I mean, why else would she settle for a man like Goderdzi?'

'What do you know?' replies another woman, staring at Manana's narrow-waisted dress with the lacy trim and satin ribbons fixed just above her pert backside.

'I just know,' says the first.

Manana stands with her back to a group of girls wearing sparkly dresses and craning their necks like hens. She throws her bouquet into the scrum. A chubby girl with red cheeks and a battle-ready look on her face emerges clutching it and breathing heavily. The other guests clap and everyone files into the dinner hall. The table is set for a banquet and piled high with food: plates of fresh herbs and *pkhali*, whole cucumbers and tomatoes nestled among bunches of enormous spring onions and radishes and dozens of other cold dishes. Avto signals to a thin man standing next to a Yamaha keyboard; a few seconds later, the nasal strains of a keyboard rendition of Mendelssohn's 'Wedding March' float across the room before being superseded by the diatonic melancholy of a Tushetian love song.

The children take their seats. Everyone is there except Irakli, who has a temperature and can't eat without bringing everything straight back up.

The toastmaster raises his voice above the hubbub: 'Dear friends, I would like to raise my glass to the bride and groom!' He presses one fleshy hand against his chest and with the other raises his glass high in the air. He looks around at the assembled guests and begins: 'Adam and Eve, my friends, were created for what? To love! To be fruitful and multiply! And as the children of Adam and Eve we too should be fruitful and multiply, as long as we do so with love! To Goderdzi and Manana – *gaumarjos*! To your union – *gaumarjos*! Bless you both. May your love for each other never fade as long as you live!'

The children pile food onto their plates: hot *khachapuri*, fried chicken, liver with walnuts, vegetable *pkhali*, walnut sauce, clay-baked *shotis puri* flatbreads and everything else that's on offer. Dali is sitting with the children, helping herself to large portions of *mchadi* cornbread and fish. Now and then she shoots a child a disapproving look, rolling her eyes and opening her grease-covered lips so wide that half-chewed mouthfuls of food almost fall out.

Dali chooses some food for Lela to take to Irakli: light, boiled dishes, nothing too rich. Lela wakes him up, but Irakli says he doesn't feel like eating. Lela touches his hot forehead, tucks him in, leaves the plate by his bed and goes back to the *supra*, where a few of the younger guests are already dancing, and fruit and cakes have been added to the table.

Lela is starting to feel the effects of the wine. 'Tiniko,' she calls over the music, 'could I have a quick word?'

Tiniko looks annoyed. She abandons her cake, stands and squeezes past the other guests to get out. Lela leads her to a corner.

'Sorry to interrupt your meal,' she says. 'I was just wondering why you took photos of Irakli. You said you'd only do the ones with no family... So I just wondered what's happened to his mother.'

'Couldn't this have waited till tomorrow, girl? Why do you care whether Irakli's got a mother or not?'

'I know he's *got* one. I've just sworn down the phone at her. She's in Greece.'

Tiniko's face softens.

'Yes,' she says, 'she's in Greece. She was really struggling here. Now she's in Greece and she won't be coming back. At least not for a long time. And once Irakli turns eighteen he can do what he pleases.' Tiniko is practically shouting to make herself heard. 'Now, I'm going back to my seat and you're not to drink any more. And what I just told you goes no further.'

The wedding party is in full swing. One of Goderdzi's cousins, an off-duty policeman, is so fired up by the music that he jumps first onto a chair and then onto the table, pulls a handgun from his waistband and fires several shots into the ceiling.

As if on cue, the music gets even louder and the children start scrabbling on the floor for the empty cartridges.

Lela and Dali give each child a piece of honey cake before herding them out of the dinner hall. Meanwhile, Avto helps the servers to drag the now-empty table back against the wall, leaving in its place a large, open dance floor.

5

Vano hates missing lessons. Even if every child in the school falls ill but one, he'll take that child into his classroom and teach them anyway. He spends his lessons pacing up and down in front of the blackboard, arms folded behind his back, a cane in one hand, recounting the lives of King David the Builder, Timur, Queen Tamar and – the children's favourite – Tsotne Dadiani, bound at the feet of his Mongol overlords, naked under the scorching sun, smeared in honey, demanding to be put to death...

Vano looks at the ground while he talks or sometimes stares into space. He never looks at the children. The teachers here are less strict than in other schools. The children find it hard to concentrate and spend most of their time during lessons talking and arguing among themselves. If the class gets so noisy that Vano can't make himself heard, he raises his cane. He used it more in the old days, back when Marcel and Ira were still at the school. Now he has neither the strength nor the inclination to threaten anyone.

Lela comes into the classroom.

'Levan, your mum's here,' she says.

Levan looks confused. He goes to the door, careful not to look too eager to run to his mum like a little boy. Lela is about to leave too when Vano calls her over.

'Take this to Gulnara, will you?'

Lela follows Vano to his desk. As soon as Vano's back is turned, the children rush to the windows to get a look at Levan's mother. Some run down to the toilets for a better vantage point and some run after Levan to watch the encounter up close.

Vano opens a drawer in his desk. Lela looks down at his long, thin hand and at the fine greying hairs on his wrist. She looks at his long fingers resting on the handle and then, in a flash, she sees herself a few years before, standing there in the history room with her knickers pulled down, her dress and jumper pushed out of the way, and Vano moving his skinny fingers down onto her hairless mound and then plunging them deeper and deeper inside her, quickly, clumsily, as if there's something within that he needs to pull but which keeps on escaping his grasp. And then, suddenly she feels pain, burning, and she grimaces but doesn't cry, not yet... Vano opens his trousers.

'Touch it. Don't be scared.'

She looks at it swaying from side to side, erect, pointing skywards. It reminds her of a skinned animal. Vano pulls her towards him.

'We'll go into town after this and I'll buy you an ice cream... You're a good girl, aren't you? Come on, you'll like it. I know you will...'

Lela puts her hand out to touch it. It feels thick in her hand, like a broom handle. She doesn't remember the next bit, just Vano standing behind her as she faces the wall. The small stool beneath her feet. Pain, right through her body, pain so fierce it burns her throat. She screams, but Vano gets angry, covers her mouth with his clammy hand, tells her off for crying, and so she stops, abruptly, and tries to do what he says. Don't say anything to anyone, he tells her, as he moves Lela's little hands back to his broom handle...

Vano takes the register out of the drawer and hands it to Lela. She looks at his withered old face, the dark circles around his eyes and his drooping, sagging mouth, and can't believe that the old man in front of her and the man with the broom handle are one and the same.

'Take this down to Gulnara,' he tells her, and turns back to his desk.

As Lela walks along the corridor she remembers the wash block, the blood running down her legs and the fear she felt when she thought she was dying.

Gulnara is on the first floor, teaching practical skills to the little ones. Lela gives her the register. There's a needle-work book lying open on the desk and Lela is so struck by the similarity between one of the geometric patterns and Gulnara's angular nose that she wonders whether that's where Gulnara got the design from.

Outside in the schoolyard, Lela feels sick. She sits on the bench in the shade of the spruce trees and lights a cigarette.

She remembers another time, in the corridor outside the gymnasium, when Vano barred her way and grabbed her hand, led her into the gym and made her take off her clothes. When she was little that happened a lot: Vano would find her, grab her hand and take her somewhere. She didn't like it, but she went anyway. Even now she can't bear people holding her hand, not even Stella, Pako or Nona. Lela remembers how damp the changing rooms were. She remembers Vano pulling her trousers off, then her tights, then her knickers, and making her stand barefoot on the cold tiled floor. She remembers too how Vaska walked in on them. How he saw Lela standing there in the changing room with no knickers. Vano, sitting on a chair with no trousers... Vano didn't see him. Vaska and Lela stared dumbly at each other, before Vaska turned and walked straight back out.

When Lela got a bit bigger, Vano stopped taking her to his classroom and the changing rooms. When Lela looks at him now she sometimes thinks maybe it never happened, maybe *that* Vano only existed in her nightmares. But when she sees Vaska and looks at the subtle smile on his face, the reality of it all shudders back through her body and the shame of that past floods her with nausea.

Lela spots Levan and his mother on a bench in the yard, talking in hushed voices. Levan's mother is an attractive woman with long auburn hair and large breasts, wearing a figure-hugging skirt and a low-cut top. Lela imagines her life to be so full of men that there's no room for her son. But even her heavy make-up can't hide the suffering on her face. She is both beautiful and broken. She gets to her feet and pulls Levan into an embrace. He hugs her back shyly,

resting his arms on her shoulders. Levan walks his mother
to the gates and she leaves. He closes the gates and runs
back towards the dormitory block without looking round,
clutching in his hand the bag full of sweets she brought
with her, thinking only of how soon he'll be eating them.
Lela watches as the woman walks slowly down the road
and signals to the driver of a passing bus. He pulls over,
opens the doors and waits, his rickety vehicle sputtering
patiently on the spot. Levan's mother gets on and travels
back to a life in disarray.

May draws to an end with a succession of rainy days.
When the rain starts pouring into the trampoline room,
Dali stands on guard to stop any children from sneaking in.
She huffs and puffs around, depositing assorted containers,
trying to outmanoeuvre the water.

Lela is on the top floor, looking down at the street
with a few other children, all staring at the downpour that
threatens to inundate the school grounds. The waters are
gushing down the road, surging through the gates and into
the yard, then flooding left and right around the buildings
as if laying siege to the school. Luckily for Lela, Tariel
has spent many rainy May days in the gatehouse and her
room is kept safe and dry by a well-maintained roof and
a slightly elevated entrance.

One afternoon the rain cascades down Kerch Street and
floods into the school grounds so fast it seems that the water
might flush away the years of accumulated grime and filth
in a single swoop. Everyone is sheltering in the TV room,

steaming up the windows by their sheer numbers. For the children, this is the closest they come to experiencing family life and togetherness. Then Tiniko walks in with Madonna, who announces that the American family has decided to adopt Irakli.

Sitting by the window with Lela, Irakli turns beetroot red.

Tiniko and Madonna have just come in out of the rain. Their soaking-wet hair lies completely flat, making their heads appear shrunken, and the contrast between this and their ample rear ends makes them look like wet chickens. They sit in the armchairs while Dali stands there crying with happiness, or maybe with grief. The children gather round. Lela shoves Irakli off the window ledge and gestures for him to join them.

'Come here, Irakli!' calls Tiniko.

Irakli squeezes through to the middle of the crowd. Levan slaps him on the shoulder and bursts into song.

'*I just called… to sa-a-a-a-y… I love you…*'

The others laugh, but they stare at Irakli as if he's just materialized in front of them. Lela looks now and finds his face completely transformed. He's stopped blushing. He perches carefully on the arm of a chair.

'Congratulations!' says Madonna enthusiastically, as if she can hardly believe this miracle herself. 'What a wonderful life you're going to have, what a future! It's a fairy tale! Providence has really smiled on you, my dear!'

She turns to face Tiniko. 'What swung it for him, do you know?'

Tiniko gives a beatific smile, as if she'd never imagined things going any other way.

'What did you say to me, Tiniko?' Madonna says dramatically. 'Let's take their photos, you said! What harm can it do, you said! Ahh, well done, Tiniko! Just imagine! If we hadn't sent that photo they might have chosen one from Yugoslavia! They've got a woman in Sarajevo, you know, she promised them a disabled child from the war! Just imagine... I mean... How old are you, boy?' she asks, turning back to Irakli.

'Nine,' says Irakli.

'You see?' Madonna shifts round to face Dali again. 'You see how quickly they changed their minds?'

Dali gazes at Irakli. 'The Americans liked the look of you, sweetheart,' she says sincerely.

Tiniko opens the window wide to let some fresh air in. The sound of rain and rushing water fills the room.

'Lela,' says Tiniko, 'well done, my dear.'

Madonna pulls a paper from her bag and addresses the room. 'Right, we've got a lot to do! We need a medical certificate, birth certificate, all the forms' – she counts the items off on her fingers, starting not with the index finger as Georgians do, but with the thumb, like an American – 'printed, signed and all that... That's for me and Tiniko to sort out, but the boy needs to do a biography and write about what he's hoping to find with his new American family...'

'I don't speak American,' says Irakli.

'First of all, it's not American, it's English. In America they speak English. And don't worry, we'll translate it for you.'

'Miss, he can barely write Georgian,' Levan pipes up. 'But I'm pretty sure he can manage *something* in English, right, Ika?' Levan elbows Irakli affectionately. '*I just called to say I love you*: that kind of thing.'

Irakli's ears go bright red.

Madonna goes on: 'The child needs to be ready to travel in September. They're coming for four days. They haven't got time to stay longer and they'll take him back with them then. It's all here, look' – Madonna waves the piece of paper – 'I mean, it's in English but I'll translate: *Dear Madonna and Tiniko. Thank you so much for the things you sent. Madonna has probably told you all about us, but we wanted to tell you ourselves what a warm, loving family this is* – I mean, you can just tell, can't you? – *We're enclosing all our paperwork and a little bit about ourselves.*'

Madonna skips ahead and starts speaking again, this time with great feeling: '*It's very hard choosing a child. We didn't want to come over to Georgia to choose. We thought it might not be good for the children and we knew how emotionally draining it would be for us too. At first we thought it would be better to go for a child no older than six because younger children find it easier to integrate and adapt, but when we saw the photo of Irakli's kind, gentle face we* –'

Madonna's chin trembles but she manages to compose herself and finishes the letter. 'Basically, seeing him was enough to change their minds.'

'Wow, Ika! They liked your ugly mug, then!' Levan pulls a face. But Dali has tears pouring down her cheeks.

It seems that the heroes of Kerch Street have not died out after all, for Irakli is destined to be one.

When the rain finally stops, Lela and Irakli go back to the gatehouse.

'What did I tell you, eh?' says Lela, cuffing Irakli on the side of the head. 'Take me with you, OK? Don't just ditch me now you're an American.'

She laughs and Irakli smiles back.

They light up a cigarette and the room fills with smoke. Lela gets up to open the tiny window.

'Lela?' says Irakli.

'Lela-Lela-Lela, what now? You won't have your Lela in America, you know! You don't need to worry, though. I'll give you Schwarzenegger's number – you can tell him I said to call.' She laughs.

'Can you take me over to use the phone?'

Lela stops. She stares at Irakli through the wisps of smoke.

'One more time, all right?' Irakli says cautiously.

'What is *wrong* with you? Why can't you just let it go?' Lela sits down at the table by the window. 'She's really got her claws into you, hasn't she? What good will calling do? You don't even know where to call!'

'Still… She might be coming back,' Irakli says calmly.

'She's never coming back! Why can't you get it into your thick head?' says Lela. She wants to say more, but stops.

Irakli sits in silence. His face seems especially thin and pale and Lela remembers what the Americans said about how kind and gentle he looked.

*

Mzia's daughter opens the door and Lela is struck once again by how much the girl's beauty spot looks like a tiny beetle. As soon as the girl sees who it is, her face clouds over and she shuts the door without a word. Lela and Irakli look at each other in surprise. Lela rings the bell again. This time Mzia opens the door. Her smile has vanished. She fixes the pair with a cold, penetrating stare.

'Hello,' says Lela. 'Sorry to bother you, but can we use your phone?'

The woman looks at them with her eyes brimming.

'Bravo!' she says suddenly. 'Bravo. Thank you *so* much for letting me do this for you!' Her voice trembles. 'I welcome you into my house and ask for nothing in return, and you come along and you use my phone whenever you want... But no, thank *you* for calling abroad and thank *you* for doing it at peak rates and getting our phone cut off. You know my husband's had to go down there to sort it all out? The poor man's just got in from work. I mean, why would you do that? Why would you take advantage like that when all I was doing was trying to help?'

Mzia is close to tears. Lela sees the beetle-girl hiding behind her mother's legs, stroking her hip and peering at Lela with one eye.

Lela and Irakli stand there in shock. Mzia shuts the door. Irakli walks back to the stairs with his head down, but Lela just stands there dumbfounded.

The door opens again, just a crack, and the beetle-girl pokes her head out and stares at them. Lela hears Mzia's voice from inside.

'Shut the door and come back inside!'

'They're still out there, Mum…'

'I said shut the door and come back in. Now!'

Lela thinks for a moment and then, to Irakli's surprise, walks over to the flat opposite, where a new family has just moved in. She rings the bell. A girl of about twelve opens the door.

'Excuse me,' says Lela, 'could we possibly use your phone for a minute? We're from the residential school. It's really important.'

The girl pulls an exaggerated glum face.

'It's not connected yet,' she says.

'Oh, OK… Sorry,' says Lela. The girl shuts the door.

Irakli sets off down the stairs but Lela rings again and when the girl opens the door she says, 'The man from the phone company's just been, you know. He was fiddling in the box downstairs. Go and have a look – he might have done yours!'

The girl goes back inside leaving the door open, walks across the hallway to a small shelf with a phone standing on it and puts the receiver to her ear.

'Oh yeah, it's working now,' she says hesitantly, as if she can't figure out who's come out on top.

Lela and Irakli go inside. The girl disappears into one of the rooms.

'Who was it?' Lela hears a woman ask.

'Kids from the special school, come to use the phone.'

Compared to Mzia's flat, this one is messy, disorganized and dark. There are no baking smells wafting from the kitchen. There's not even a chair to sit on. Irakli unfolds a small piece of paper with a phone number on it in Lela's handwriting. He dials. An old lady answers in Greek. After a few minutes, unable to make herself understood, she shouts down the phone, 'No Inga! No Inga! Inga no live here any more!'

Irakli rings Ivlita. Ivlita doesn't know anything. Inga hasn't called her. Ivlita assumes she's moved house.

Irakli walks back beside Lela with his head down. Lela feels deflated too. The look of betrayal on Mzia's face has left a bad taste in her mouth.

'You go ahead,' Lela says suddenly. 'I'll be back in a bit.'

'Where are you going? Can I come?'

'No. You go ahead and I'll be along in a bit.'

'Fine.'

Irakli shrugs and carries on walking towards the school with his hands in his pockets.

Lela heads back to the tower block but this time to a different floor. She rings a doorbell and Marika answers. She smiles, surprised to see Lela.

'Hey. How are you?'

'Can I talk to you for a sec?'

'What is it?'

Lela takes the same small piece of paper out of her pocket and reads out something scribbled on it in her handwriting.

'*Inga no live here any more*. What does that mean?'

Marika stares at Lela for a moment, then looks at the piece of paper and tells her.

'You know Irakli? He's being adopted by an American couple. They're coming to get him in September. What I wanted to ask you is whether you could teach him a bit of English. You speak English, right?'

'Well, I have lessons, but I'm not very good. He'd be better off with a proper teacher.'

'You can be his teacher. I'll pay. How much do you pay for yours?'

'Um, I pay monthly and I go twice a week…'

'We'll pay monthly too and come twice a week. Or you can come to us twice a week. I've got my own room so that's all fine, and you can just teach him a few bits and bobs so he's not completely clueless when he gets there.'

'I dunno… I've got exams coming up and I'm really busy. I'm applying to university soon…'

'We'll pay. How much do you pay a month?'

Marika doesn't answer.

'We've got money,' Lela says. 'I've got a job, haven't I, looking after the cars. It's not much, but it might be enough.'

'OK, fine. I pay forty *lari*. She's a friend of the family… How about half that?'

'Twenty?' Lela asks.

The girls fall silent. Marika stares at Lela, and Lela stares back and thinks how strange it is that they once put their hands inside each other's knickers. She can still recall the scent it left on her fingers.

Marika takes a deep breath as if she's had enough of haggling and asks, 'Does that work for you?'

'Yeah, twenty's fine.'

'Good. I'll come twice a week, but it'll have to be early afternoon cos I've got tutors every evening.'

'How much per lesson, then? So we can pay as we go along.'

'Twenty divided by two, that's ten *lari* for two weeks, so one week'll be five. Look, let's make it just once a week, that suits me better,' says Marika.

'You're the best. When can you come?'

'Tomorrow at two?'

'OK,' says Lela. She starts running down the stairs.

'Wait!' Marika calls after her. She stands at the top looking down at Lela. 'Will he do the work?'

Lela thinks for a moment, then shouts back, 'He'll do it!'

The next day Lela and Irakli meet Marika in the gate-house. Irakli is sitting at the table with a thin notebook and a pen laid out in front of him. Marika sits down opposite him.

'*Hello*,' says Marika, and looks expectantly at Irakli.

Irakli looks at Lela. Lela shrugs.

'*Hello* is like *gamarjoba*. It's what you say to greet some-one. Let's practise. I'll greet you and you greet me back.'

Irakli nods.

'*Hello*,' says Marika.

'*Hello*,' Irakli parrots back at her.

'*Perfect*,' says Marika, and translates that too.

Lela stays for the lesson. Irakli learns a few English words and then writes them in his notebook. It soon becomes apparent that Irakli has either forgotten, can't write or simply never knew several letters of the Georgian alphabet. Marika changes tack, deciding that Irakli needs to practise this first. Lela objects, but Marika convinces her that he'll never learn another language if he can't write his own.

'If he tries to learn everything by heart, teaching him will be a nightmare,' says Marika, scratching her nose. 'How can he write stuff down if he doesn't know his letters?'

With Lela's help, Irakli writes out all thirty-three letters of the Georgian alphabet in his notebook. By the time he gets to the final letter, one so rarely used that Marika has to guide his little hand to help him with the shape, Irakli is exhausted. The lesson is over. Irakli says he has a headache, and Lela gives Marika five *lari*.

Marika steps out of the gatehouse into a crowd of children.

'*I just called to say I love you*,' Levan shouts out.

Marika can't help smiling.

'Do you even know what it means?' she asks him.

Levan blushes.

'I love you,' says Marika. '*Miqvarkhar*.'

Marika's words cause uproar. The children start shrieking with laughter and Levan pulls a face like he's sucking a lemon.

Lela comes out of the gatehouse.

'Clear off, Levan. Leave the poor girl alone, will you?'

'Oh, leave him. He's all right,' says Marika.

'Anyway, why would I clear off now? She's just told me she loves me,' Levan says, and the children start laughing again.

The bell rings and everyone runs to the dinner hall. Irakli mutters to himself as he goes, '*Perfect! Perfect!*'

Lela looks at what's on the table: boiled potatoes and cutlets. Not meat cutlets but the fake cutlets made from various types of stale bread, onion and herbs, dipped in flour and fried. Next to them there's a three-litre bottle of sour fruit sauce and some watered-down tomato paste with bits of onion floating in it. The children pounce on the sauce, pouring it out of the bottle straight onto their plates. Lela helps herself to a single cutlet, puts the whole thing in her mouth at once, chews and swallows. She gets up and goes outside.

She lights a cigarette and walks along the path that borders the pear field. She wanders around the side of the building and stops by the steps in front of the dormitory block. Everyone is still in the dinner hall. Lela flicks the cigarette butt into a corner and goes inside. She heads up to the top floor and walks towards the trampoline room. She's still some distance away when she notices that the door is open. She goes inside and sees Vaska standing with his back to her in the doorway where the balcony once was, looking down at the ground. He doesn't notice her come in. She tiptoes over, grabs his top with both hands and gives him a good hard shake.

'Boo!'

Terrified, Vaska throws his arms out instinctively, like a bird about to take flight. He manages to regain his balance and spins round to face Lela. They fall on each other, arms raised, like two rams locking horns, and grapple long and hard. Vaska grimaces, flushed with exertion. He looks like he's about to start crying. Lela is spent. Suddenly, simultaneously, they let go. Gasping for breath, they collapse on the beds.

'What's the matter, did I scare you?' Lela asks, barely able to catch her breath.

Vaska straightens his clothes.

'What were you looking at down there, huh? You'll have a much better view when you fall out and smash your head on the concrete. What are you doing in here anyway? Why did you open the door?'

Vaska stands and walks towards the door.

'It was already open,' he says, staring back at Lela. She holds his gaze; his face is calmer now and the smile that was absent during their fight is back.

'It was open, was it?' Lela sounds doubtful. 'Don't come the innocent with me.'

'It was open,' Vaska says again.

'What about the padlock?'

'Nope.'

Lela looks at him. His smile is really starting to get on her nerves.

'What are you smirking for?'

'Smirking? Me?'

'No, me. You're an idiot, you know that?' She sighs. 'Don't you want any dinner? Hurry up or you'll be too late.'

'I'm not hungry,' says Vaska.

'You know, I can't work you out,' Lela says. 'What are you doing in a special school anyway? Are you *actually* a moron or do you just act like one?'

'What, me?'

'No, me.'

Vaska says nothing. He simply turns around and walks off. Lela watches him go, still waiting for an answer.

'Don't let me catch you up here again, Vaska, or I'll break both your legs.'

Vaska disappears down the corridor.

6

I'm going to kill Vano before winter, Lela thinks to her-self. *It's summer now. Plenty of time. Irakli's leaving in September and once he's gone I'll kill Vano. By the end of winter. After that it might be too late. He's so old he might just die, all by himself...*

Lela can't bear the thought. She vows to herself that Vano will not have a natural death.

It's a sunny day and there's a pleasant breeze outside. Lela is sitting on the landing at the top of the fire escape, thinking about the winter when she, Irakli, Levan and Vaska stole firewood from the neighbour's shed. The owner had caught them in there. He'd locked the shed door and threatened to call the police. He got a bit physical too. Irakli started crying. Levan was too frightened to speak. Vaska, though, gathered all the courage he could muster and said, 'We were so cold we've just burned our shoes and now there's nothing left to burn! That's why we're stealing from you!'

The neighbour was a gruff, hard-working man who never looked anyone in the eye and had little interest in talking to others, but Vaska's words had seemed to mollify him. He opened the shed door wide and stared long and hard at the children standing in the moonlight, before loading them up with as much dry wood as they could carry and letting them go. He watched them leave, shaking his head. The children had crept back to the yard, squeezed through the fence, dropped the firewood and heaved a sigh of relief. They had found Stella sitting by the fence, crying, waiting for their safe return.

They were warm that night. Lela felt herself warming a little towards Vaska too. Not that she said anything. She didn't even give him a smile. She just let him sit by the stove and talk.

I'll move out this winter, thinks Lela, basking in the sun. Once she's killed Vano she'll just grab her bag and go. To somewhere more central, maybe. She has a couple of classmates on Lotkin Street. Maybe she'll stay with them for a while. Or go and find Yana. Or catch a train west, as a last resort. To Batumi, maybe. She could look for Marcel. She's sure everyone will know Marcel. They're probably all afraid of him. First she'll track down Marcel and then she'll head for the beach. Just the thought of seeing the sea makes her giddy. She can't swim, but she'll learn.

Every June, the cherry tree in Tariel's garden produces enormous red fruit, and every year Tariel waits patiently for it to ripen. He takes some home to eat fresh and some to stew and preserve, and the rest he takes out to the road to sell. He drags an old wooden table out of the courtyard and stands buckets of cherries on top. If it's really hot he plants three poles in the ground and makes himself a sunshade with an old cotton sheet. He gets a good price for his cherries and he doesn't like to haggle.

This cherry tree has caused no end of trouble over the years. From day one, Tariel has struggled to keep the local kids away. He bought a sheepdog. Then one of the children hid a needle in its meat and the dog died right there in the yard in front of Tariel's eyes. On another occasion he ran out with his hunting rifle to scare some children out of the tree. He fired a shot into the air and one fell and broke both legs. His wife has been begging him to cut it down ever since, but Tariel won't hear of it. He just watches patiently as the clusters of cherries burst forth among the oval leaves, and swell and finally ripen. Lela used to steal fruit from Tariel's tree but he caught her once and tore a strip off her. Since then she's steered well clear.

Lela and Irakli are on their way to buy cigarettes from the kiosk. They walk past Tariel's fence.

'Lela, the cherries are ripe,' says Irakli.

'If they're ripe Tariel will take care of them. They won't stay uneaten,' she replies.

Irakli gazes through the fence at the branches rustling in the breeze and the foliage shifting to reveal clusters of luscious red fruit.

Every now and then old women emerge to empty buckets of water in front of their gates, as if that will somehow cool the air, leaving passers-by to marvel at how clean and tidy their houses must be if they have time to sweep and rinse off the bare earth outside.

Irakli sighs.

'How can I go to America without tasting Tariel's cherries?'

That evening Lela gathers Irakli, Levan, Vaska and Stella in the gatehouse and reveals that they're going to steal Tariel's cherries later that night.

Tariel now has a large mixed-breed dog called Bandit, a stocky, hairy beast with a square head, broad muzzle, kind eyes and enormous paws. As far as Tariel is concerned, he's good for nothing. Bandit knows everyone in the street and every child at the school. He attacks nothing and nobody, just lopes around and sprawls in the sun. The neighbourhood cats walk so close that their tails touch his nose and he simply lies there, unruffled.

At three o'clock the next morning Lela goes up to wake Stella. She is out of bed like a shot, still in her clothes from the night before, half asleep but ready for the task at hand. They tiptoe down the stairs. Irakli, Levan and Vaska are waiting in the dark gatehouse.

Together, they steal out of the yard, their shadows creeping behind them, elongated black bodies that drift slightly to one side as if trying to pull away but compelled by the moon to follow wherever their masters go. It's a hot night; the breeze wafting through the branches of the trees is almost imperceptible. They stop by Tariel and

Narcissa's gate. Lela climbs onto the fence and calls softly into the yard.

'Bandit!'

The gormless mutt pads towards the fence, wagging his tail. Lela climbs back down, pokes her hand through and unhooks a length of twisted wire to open the gate. Bandit sticks his muzzle through the gap. While Lela strokes his nose, Stella grabs his collar and hauls him outside.

'Here, Bandit. Come on, boy,' she says affectionately.

Irakli helps her tie a rope to his collar.

'Tariel names this soft sod Bandit, but that witch he's married to is named after a flower? Where's the justice?' says Levan.

'Take him well away from here, and not down by Suliko's either or he'll set the dogs off. OK, Stella?'

'I know,' whispers Stella, and crosses confidently over the moonlit road, holding Bandit tightly by the collar. She's wearing Nona's pink frilly dress and it flutters as she runs. Bandit whimpers happily, enjoying his night-time excursion.

Lela goes into Tariel's garden and beckons the boys to follow.

'When you spit out the stones make sure they don't land on the garage,' she hisses. 'And if I whistle, you just leg it, OK?' she says, tucking her T-shirt into her trousers. She tightens her belt. The boys do the same.

'We should get some for Stella first, right?' asks Irakli.

'If she gets cherries from all of us she'll also be getting the shits,' says Levan, and the other boys snigger.

'Button it, smart-arse,' Lela responds.

She closes the gate from inside. Now that their eyes are used to the dark they can clearly make out Tariel's tidy front yard and a simple brick house with a glass door covered by a curtain on the inside. Lela picks her way across the garden towards Tariel's cherry tree.

Lela decides to send the smallest child up first. She and Vaska give Irakli a leg-up; he hauls himself into the tree and disappears into the darkness. Then Lela gives Levan the nod and he steps carefully onto their interlocked fingers. He hops straight up, hugs the trunk tightly and inches up into the branches until, like Irakli, he's swallowed up by the blackness.

Only Lela and Vaska are left on the ground.

'You go,' Vaska whispers, and crouches down so she can step up onto his back.

Lela pushes off with one foot and pulls herself straight up into the tree. She presses her cheek against the rough bark and closes her eyes. She hugs the trunk like a lover, and the tree just stands there, transfixed save for a slight sway as the wind combs through its branches. Finally Vaska too throws his arms and legs around the trunk and works his way slowly upwards. He grabs a branch with one hand, swings his body over and hangs there like a long, thin monkey.

The cherry tree sways a little under the weight of its nocturnal plunderers but stands firm in the ground; like a mother welcoming hungry children, it caresses them and whispers invocations to protect them from the evil eye. There's a sudden rustle of leaves and the loud crack of a branch breaking under someone's foot. Everyone freezes, but the only sound they can hear is the crickets' chirping under the fence.

They cram their T-shirts with cherries, tearing off handful after handful, leaves and all, stuffing them down between the fabric and their bare skin. They eat some there and then too. Somebody spits out a stone and it bounces off the slate roof with a loud ping. Everyone freezes for a second time, but again nothing happens.

Lela edges out along one of the branches to try to reach one that is heavy with fruit, but finds Vaska already wrestling with it. They stare at each other. Lela studies Vaska's smiling face in the moonlight. He leans back with his full weight to try and pull the branch closer so that Lela can reach it. She grabs it with one hand but it's thick and strong. Vaska grabs hold with both hands, giving Lela the time she needs. She's in no rush; she twists off the bunches of cherries, tastes them and throws the stones far away over the garage roof. She fires a few at Vaska, blowing them into his face. He just turns his face slightly to the side so that for a moment he's lost to Lela in the shade of the leaves, until she finds those hazel eyes again, staring back at her. Lela picks every single fruit from the branch as if she's testing how long Vaska can hold on, then at last she lets go and moves to another branch. She pulls a thin, flexible branch towards her and lets go. It whips at Vaska's face and Vaska fends it off.

They slip quietly back through the gate, their T-shirts stuffed full of cherries. Stella is on the other side of the road, walking Bandit up and down. She runs across to her friends.

The moon is so bright it could almost be daytime. Stella unties the rope from the dog's collar, gives him a stroke and pushes him back through the open gate.

Lela closes the gate.

A few minutes later they're back on school grounds. They climb the fire escape and sit at the top, three on the landing, two on the step below. Stella opens out the skirt of her pink dress and Lela fills it with cherries from inside her T-shirt. Stella's eyes gleam with delight.

'Bandit was such a good boy. He didn't make a sound,' she says proudly, and spits her cherry stone towards the spruce trees.

'He's a clever boy, Bandit. Not like Vaska. First he broke that branch, then he landed that cherry stone smack bang in the middle of the garage roof,' says Lela, and everyone laughs. 'Bringing him along was asking for trouble,' she says teasingly.

Vaska says nothing.

'Ika,' Stella blurts out suddenly, 'will you think about us when you're in America?'

'Of course he will,' says Levan, cos he'll be so miserable, won't he, crying himself to sleep every night: Stella, I want Stellaaaaaa…'

Stella giggles excitedly.

'I just can't imagine myself in America. I keep thinking none of this is real,' Irakli says pensively.

'You keep thinking that, son. Thinking it doesn't make it true, though,' says Levan.

'Don't you ever get tired?' Lela asks in bemusement.

'I most certainly do not! Take me along to those English lessons, Lela, and just watch how hard I work!'

He elbows Stella.

'Oi, Stella, tell them where you're going to work when you grow up!'

'I don't want to,' Stella says, looking embarrassed.

'The poor girl said it *one time* and you're still taking the piss?' says Vaska.

'Go on, Stella, tell Lela!' Levan urges.

Stella gives a deep sigh. 'I'm going to work at the College of Light Industry.'

The boys start laughing hysterically. Stella looks offended.

'Where have you got that idea from, Stella?' Lela asks her.

Stella just sighs again.

'Dali was talking about this girl with no family who started working at the College of Light Industry, and cos Stella just parrots everything, doesn't she, so…'

'Hey, I'm not a parrot,' shouts Stella, and Lela glares at her. 'He's a parrot! Tell him, Lela!'

'OK, OK, just keep your voice down,' Lela says gently.

'Oi, Stella!' Levan continues. 'You know what they say about the girls who work there, right? "If you want a real pro," they say, "get yourself a girl from the College of Light Industry." Oh yes, those girls do the best job in town!'

Even Lela can't help laughing.

'Cos it's where the whores go, isn't it? Real *pros*, best *job* in town, d'you get it?'

Stella looks forlorn.

'Shut up!' she whines. 'Lela, tell him that's not true!'

'OK, OK, it's not true,' Lela says reassuringly.

'Stella, love,' giggles Levan, 'don't bring shame on us! Don't start working there or how will Irakli ever be able to look the Americans in the eye!'

'Oh, for God's sake, Levan!' Stella snaps. 'Just pack it in, will you?'

She narrows her eyes, ready for Levan's next insult, but it never comes. He just claps his hands together triumphantly and laughs.

Eventually Stella falls asleep, there on the top step. Irakli gives her a shake but he can't wake her.

Lela picks Stella up. They make their way slowly down the fire escape and back to the dormitory block. Moonlight is streaming into the yard through the spruce trees; it looks as if the ground is covered in a light dusting of snow.

The boys follow Lela up to the girls' dormitory. Lela lays Stella on the bed, pulls the covers over her and stares at the cherry leaf she's clutching.

She goes back out to where Levan, Vaska and Irakli are waiting in the corridor, passing round a cigarette. They leave the last few drags for Lela.

When they reach the floor below they say goodnight and the boys go back to their dormitory. Lela goes downstairs and over to the gatehouse. She collapses onto her bed fully dressed.

*

The next day the sweet taste of Tariel's cherries quickly sours when they hear that Tariel has shot Bandit with his hunting rifle. Stella starts to cry. Tariel emerges with a spade and Bandit's corpse in a wheelbarrow. Lela intercepts him and offers to bury Bandit. Tariel, who seems to have aged overnight, eyes Lela suspiciously, then sets down the wheelbarrow and says, 'Bring it back to my yard. And don't lose my spade.'

Bandit's nocturnal companions dig him a grave on the little mound between the wash block and the playground. The other children stand close by and watch as they bury him. While the boys tread down the earth covering poor Bandit's grave, Stella picks dandelions and buttercups, then lays them on the ground. Teary-eyed, distraught, she also seems suddenly wiser, like someone party to a new and terrible truth.

Lela rolls the wheelbarrow back to Tariel's as promised. She takes Stella along. When they reach the road, she scoops Stella up and sits her in the wheelbarrow, gives her the spade and takes off fast as if Stella's just slammed her foot on the gas pedal. The force throws Stella backwards but she somehow stays upright and laughs giddily. She sits up in the wheelbarrow wielding the spade like a canoeist navigating rapids. She plunges her spade-paddle into the waves, her expression a mixture of fear and exhilaration.

It's tougher going upstream. When they reach Kerch Street, Stella jumps out of her boat and the two of them struggle together against the flow. The air feels thick and heavy, as if the sky and clouds are pressing down, driving the birds out of the heavens.

'It's gonna rain,' says Lela, watching the sparrows flying just above the asphalt, circling conspiratorially before coming briefly to rest and then, sensing danger, soaring up as one into the air and speeding away.

Narcissa meets them at the gate. She takes the boat and paddle back without a word and offers Lela a two-*lari* coin.

'We don't want any money, but thank you,' says Lela.

'We don't want money,' echoes Stella.

As they're walking back to the school the heavens open. They make a dash for it. Stella instinctively grabs Lela's hand, but Lela breaks free, preferring to run side by side without touching, like sparrows flying in their murmur.

They run in to the school, soaked to the skin. The other children are nowhere to be seen.

Stella exclaims crossly, 'I bet they're on the trampolines!'

They run upstairs, Stella struggling to keep up, breathless but determined, proud to be helping Lela.

They reach the trampoline room. The door is unlocked. There's no one in the corridor but they can hear the squeak of the bed frames inside. Stella raises her eyebrows high and looks sternly at Lela, as if she can't believe anyone has this much temerity. Lela puts her finger to her lips and peeks inside: water is dripping heavily from the ceiling and there in the middle of the room, jumping up and down on one of the beds, panting, sweating, oblivious to everything, is Irakli. Lela catches brief snippets of English, phrases from his lessons with Marika: *I am fine! My name is Irakli!*

Tucked out of sight in the doorway, Lela and Stella stare. On the other side of the non-existent balcony door the rain comes down in a solid curtain.

'*I am fine!*' Irakli shouts again.

Lela quietly pulls the door to. She shakes her head to tell Stella to stay quiet. They go back downstairs.

'Stella, just because I didn't say anything to Irakli doesn't mean you can go up there, OK?' says Lela.

'I know, I know,' answers Stella, and runs towards the dormitory to change her clothes. 'I mean, he won't be able to jump around like that in America, will he?'

'No,' says Lela. 'He won't.'

Irakli doesn't have English class the next day. Marika sends one of her neighbour's kids over to tell Lela she's got a bad stomach ache.

Irakli is delighted.

'Must be her time of the month,' he says.

Lela gives him a swift clip round the ear.

'You don't have to repeat *everything* you hear, you know!'

After dinner, Irakli and Lela walk over to the pear field. The air smells fresh and clean after the night's rain. Apart from the chatter of the birds in the trees there's not a sound to be heard. The grass is a lush, vibrant green. Lela walks along the path around the field, smoking. Irakli walks by her side.

'Lela,' he says suddenly, 'I think Vaska likes you.'

'Pack it in, will you?'

'I'm not just saying it to wind you up.'

'You know what?' says Lela quietly, taking one last drag, 'I think it's *you* Vaska likes, not me, and if you're not careful I'm going to marry you off to him. You can have Stella as your dowry. Actually, no, she's too good for you. You can have Dali or Tiniko instead.'

Irakli sighs. 'There's just no talking to you sometimes.'

Lela throws the cigarette butt away and stares across the field at the pear trees. Their gnarled, twisting branches are hanging low after the heavy rain.

'Fine, you don't believe me. Look how much crap he takes from you, though. I wouldn't put up with it, that's for sure.'

'He puts up with it cos he's scared of me, isn't he, little gypsy chickenshit.'

'He's not scared of you, Lela. Vaska's not scared of anyone. Remember when that boy came to play football, that big lad, and was calling us retards and then he told Vaska to go fuck himself… Remember what Vaska did to him?'

Lela thinks for a moment.

'Go and get me a pear, will you?'

'I can bring you one, but you're not gonna eat it, are you?'

'Just get me one anyway.'

Irakli takes off his shoes and socks and rolls up his trouser legs. When he gets to the middle of the field he calls back to Lela, 'Which tree shall I get it from? If I fall over and drown out here it'll be your fault, you know.'

'Don't worry, you're not going to drown.'

'What about this one?' he asks, pointing to a branch heavy with fruit.

'Fine.'

Irakli looks at the large, round, green pears. He grabs hold of one and pulls it off. Holding his arms out to the side, he walks back across the field and onto dry land, carrying Lela's pear. His legs are caked in mud up to his knees. Irakli tosses Lela the pear. She catches it, wipes it on her trousers and sinks her teeth in.

'Nope, no good,' she says, and offers it to Irakli.

'If they were any good there'd be none left on the tree!' says Irakli, taking a tiny bite anyway. He shudders, leans back and then throws the pear back into the field as hard as he can.

7

In mid-July, the heat is so stifling that it drives the residents indoors to hide from the sun. The neighbourhood rumour mill threatens to grind to a halt. Nevertheless, word trickles through from the flats next door that Manana has left Goderdzi. Everyone has their own theory. Some claim that in fact he threw her out when certain rumours got back to him. Some doubt Manana was a virgin when they married. Others are sure it's because Goderdzi is impotent. Whatever the reason, the lovely Manana packs her two suitcases and prepares to leave Kerch Street for ever.

Her father arrives to collect her. He wedges his daughter's suitcases into the back of his Lada and calmly shuts the boot. Manana's wavy black hair hangs loose and the proud smile she wore on her wedding day has disappeared without a trace. She is pale, but the neighbours can't help noticing how beautiful she is nonetheless. Goderdzi is hiding indoors. Venera pokes her head out of a ground-floor window and passes Manana the fur coat she'd left in the wardrobe. It seems there's no chance she'll be back for the winter. Things appear amicable enough: Manana's father and Venera are behaving so sensitively, so affably, that anyone passing would assume the young woman was just off on a short trip.

Manana gets into the car without saying goodbye to her mother-in-law. Her father goes over to the window.

'Goodbye, then, Venera. Take care,' he says softly.

Venera doesn't reply. She looks sadly at the man taking her beautiful Manana away for ever. Nobody knows better than Venera that you don't let a girl like Manana walk out of your life, but what can she do? Manana winds down the window to get some air as the car pulls out of the yard. She doesn't look back at Venera standing there forlornly.

A month later Venera hires the dinner hall again. Goderdzi is getting remarried, this time through a match-maker, to a refugee from Abkhazia.

The whole school, needless to say, does what it can to support Venera, who seems to want to put her son's first marriage behind her as quickly as possible and, more importantly, to ensure that her neighbours forget about it too.

The next day in the courtyard, as Goderdzi lies flat on his back under his car surrounded by other young men, Lela walks past Koba and – quietly, so no one can hear – says, 'I need to see you.'

They meet at the end of Kerch Street. Lela opens the car door and gets in. Koba seems pleased; he drives off, heading out of town along the Tianeti Highway. Lela looks out of the window at the road, the houses, the dogs sprawled on the carriageway, at the handful of people walking along, strangers who have no idea that, at that very moment, Koba is taking Lela to the woods. The thought makes her happy.

Koba turns off the main road onto a narrow dirt track. There are cornfields to the left and right, nothing but green as far as the eye can see, and up ahead an empty track which skirts a low mound, where a red-brown cow stands grazing, before rising in the distance and disappearing into the forest.

Koba starts getting undressed. He's not wearing the palm trees today but a blue-and-black checked shirt with a white T-shirt underneath. He's thin and bony. He takes off his jeans and lays them on the back seat.

'Take your clothes off,' he tells Lela. She stubs her cigarette out carefully, tucks what's left into the front pocket of her shirt and starts to undress.

By now Koba is sitting in just his pants and socks. His pants are sticking up in the middle, as if they're stretched taut over a cone. Koba pulls a condom out of his wallet. Lela's half undressed, wearing only her T-shirt and knickers. She lowers the seat back. Koba tugs at her knickers, grunts at her to take them off. He takes off his pants and rolls the condom onto his cock. Skinned animal, thinks Lela. She's still got one foot in her knickers when Koba shoves his cock in its little latex coat inside her and groans. Koba starts moving, then yanks Lela's T-shirt up and kneads away at her left breast as if he's trying to get dough off his fingers. He's starting to sweat. Lela tries to match his rhythm so he'll come quickly but Koba doesn't like it. He wants to be the only one controlling the in-and-out, in-and-out. Lela's got her legs up high in the air, the soles of her feet pressed against the roof fabric, and she's taken by surprise when Koba lunges at her lips and presses his enormous mouth against hers. She feels his cold lips and his wet tongue flapping around in her mouth like a dying fish. She feels strange, her stomach tightens, she wraps her feet around Koba's sweaty back and starts to rock her hips. Koba gets even more excited, but he still won't let Lela move. He tears his lips away from hers and grabs a foot in each hand. His movements become more frenzied. Lela doesn't resist. Any desire to move evaporates; the heat in her stomach fades away. With a couple of thrusts of his skinny rump Koba comes, gives a roar and collapses like a deadweight onto Lela.

A few minutes later they're dressed again and in the car, heading back down the road towards Tbilisi. The light's fading. Outside, a handful of people stand with their bags, waiting for a bus, and in that moment Lela thinks this is probably how a husband and wife would sit in their car when they're heading back in fading light to children waiting at home.

Koba stops the car some distance from the school and gives Lela five *lari*.

Lela walks away, smoking a cigarette. She goes into the gatehouse, lies down and is deeply asleep within minutes.

Irakli has his next lesson in the gatehouse again. Lela seems out of sorts, sprawled on the bed, motionless and staring at the ceiling.

Irakli's eyes are bloodshot. At almost every English lesson recently he's complained of a headache.

'So, tell me again how you'd say that you want something to eat.'

'You'd say, *I'm hungry* or *I'm starvy*.'

'*Starving*.'

'Yeah,' replies Irakli.

'Good. Now let's practise some vocab,' says Marika.

Irakli sighs deeply and gives Lela a look that says he can't take much more.

'Hey, you know what?' Lela sits bolt upright. 'Can't you teach him some proper vocab?'

'What do you mean, "proper vocab"?' Marika asks.

Irakli perks up. 'Swear words,' he offers.

'You know, the really useful stuff. Like… What's the English for, er… *manhood*?' Lela coughs pointedly.

Irakli snorts. Lela lets it go. Marika blushes.

'It's *dick*,' she says, sounding bemused.

'What?' says Lela, not expecting an answer that quickly.

'Yeah, it's *dick*,' says Marika confidently.

'Can you call someone that too?' Lela asks, laughing. 'Like, *Shut up, dick!*'

'Why would he want to?' asks Marika.

'He just would, all right? If he doesn't need to, he won't, but if he *does* need to he's hardly going to phone us from the States to ask how, is he? Let's just teach him now!'

'I'm not really sure…' Marika ponders. '*Piss off, you dick*… That might work, I guess. I dunno. I never learned to swear, never needed to. I only know that one because a guy in my class kept asking if I wanted to see his *dick-tionary*... I can ask around, if you really want to know. I know some people.'

'We do want to know. He can learn *dog* and *cat* when he's over there – we should be teaching him what to say so that nobody gives him a hard time!'

'OK, fine. What else?' says Marika, tearing a sheet from Irakli's notebook and holding her pen at the ready.

Irakli comes alive. Here, at last, is something to make it all worthwhile.

'OK,' says Lela, sitting cross-legged on the bed and staring out of the window. 'Have you got *Piss off, you dick* down?'

'Yeah, got that.'

'Then how about something like, "Get your hands off me, you old tramp."'

'Oh, God,' Marika says, laughing. 'Do they even *have* tramps in America? I'll have to see what I can do with that one.'

'And find out how you'd threaten to tear someone a new arsehole if they don't leave you alone.'

Irakli giggles. Marika notes it down.

'Oh, what about...' says Irakli, desperate to contribute something to his emergency phrasebook but unable to think of anything rude enough. 'How would I ask someone not to kidnap me or, er –'

'Wait,' Lela interrupts. 'Make it something about break-ing every bone in their body, one by one.'

Marika writes it down.

'I wouldn't actually go round saying this stuff in America, though. Things are different over there. It's not like Georgia.'

'Just keep writing. He'll use it if he needs it. Have you ever heard him swear?'

'No...'

'And you think that means he doesn't know any swear words? He swears like a trooper when he needs to, and good for him! Or do you want people to push him around?'

'OK, fine,' says Marika, and carries on writing. 'Break every bone... one by one...'

'There you go!' says Lela. 'That'll do for now. We'll think of some more later.'

Marika gets up to go. Lela gives her five *lari*. She still owes her ten for the last two weeks, but promises to pay her back soon.

Madonna comes to visit. The children swarm around her like bees around a walking beehive.

Dali rushes off to look for Lela and Irakli. She arrives at the door of the gatehouse completely out of breath, throws it open and exclaims, 'Madonna's here!'

Standing in the doorway, her wild hair silhouetted against the sun, Dali looks like some outlandish pear-shaped fairy-tale character.

'Come on,' she says. 'The Americans have sent photos!' Then she spins around and dashes off again. For just a moment, Dali looks like one of the children, running at full tilt to embrace a moment of joy amid the monotony of her daily existence.

Lela throws her shoes on and she and Irakli race after Dali.

In Tiniko's office they find Tiniko, Madonna, Dali and a large group of children poring over the photos, which Madonna has arranged on her ample lap.

'Look, Irakli, it's your new parents! Your mum, there, and your dad,' says Madonna.

Dali starts crying. The photo shows a couple standing in front of a carefully manicured lawn: a tall man with greying hair, a large moustache and a sincere smile, wearing jeans and a white T-shirt, and a broad-hipped woman with a wide smile and straight grey hair hanging loose on her shoulders, wearing a long, colourful skirt and a white shirt.

'That's them! That's John and Deborah,' says Madonna gleefully. '*Such* good people, you simply *cannot* imagine! I spoke to some journalists and they're going to come and talk to you – they were *ever* so interested! And the Ministry are just *beside* themselves! They're being *ever* so helpful...'

'Well, Irakli? Do you like the look of Deborah and John, dear?' asks Dali.

'I guess.'

Lela stares down at John and Deborah, at their faces, their clothes and their lawn. Right at the edge of the photo she can see the front end of a car.

'Is that their car?' she asks.

'I don't know,' Madonna says dismissively, and pulls out another photo. This one shows the rest of John and Deborah's family, adult children who, according to Madonna, already have their own homes. The next few photos are of other children John and Deborah have raised, and who look like neither their parents nor each other. The first few are white and fair-haired, but then comes a photo of a young black man wearing a black gown and a strange-looking hat, looking directly into the camera and flashing a broad toothy grin. The children burst out laughing.

'Jesus Christ!' exclaims Levan.

The children are in hysterics. Madonna tries to explain what's happening in the photograph but nobody can hear her above the din. Lela catches enough to work out that this is John and Deborah's adopted son on his high school graduation day.

I bet he got a gold medal too, thinks Lela, remembering Kirile.

Koba and Lela meet at the bottom of Kerch Street. Koba doesn't want anyone to see him with a girl from the School for Idiots. He takes back roads the whole way there and he tells her to duck down when they see someone he knows.

The sun has been beating down all day but when Koba drives out of the city a cool breeze rushes in and cuts through the heat of the car.

Lying there with her legs open, Lela hears the crickets chirping and thinks that maybe somebody's coming. She props herself up on her elbows while Koba looks around until he's satisfied nobody's there. Lela lies back down, wraps her legs around Koba and moves with his rhythm. Koba tries to take control. Almost instinctively Lela grabs one of Koba's skinny buttocks and pulls him into her, harder, and feels that warmth in her stomach, and her entire body as one, a bundle of fibres, a balloon full of water sloshing gently back and forth, back and forth, until the warmth floods out of her stomach and through her whole body, and she grips his buttock hard and lets out a sudden cry. Deeply aroused, Koba stares down at her, a drop of sweat hanging off the end of his nose, then surrenders to the ecstasy and comes.

Lela gets out of the car and goes into the field to pee. She doesn't hurry back. Returning to the car, she finds Koba dressed, standing by the driver's door, smoking. Lela asks for a cigarette.

They sit in the car in silence. Koba takes a five-*lari* note out of his jean pocket and hands it to Lela.

'I don't want it,' she says briskly.

Koba looks at her in surprise.

'I don't want it,' she repeats.

Her face is flushed and her hair, wet with sweat, hangs down over her forehead. Koba sees a hint of a smile on her face.

'I came too, didn't I?'

Koba slaps Lela across the face with the back of his hand and splits her lip. She cries out in pain and covers her face with her hand.

'You're not right in the head, you know that? Get out of the car!'

123

Lela opens the door with one hand, the other one still pressed over her mouth, and gets out. Koba throws the five-*lari* note at her and slams the door. He backs out of the field, leaving Lela standing there on the dirt track surrounded by corn.

The sound of the car fades. Lela picks up the five-*lari* note and shoves it into her pocket. The crickets are chirping more loudly now. It's dusk and the entire landscape has a bluish hue. A light breeze dances across the field and Lela can hear the sound of the sea in the rustling corn. She picks up her pace. Back at the road, she waits to flag down a car.

After a short time a white Lada 4x4 stops for her. The driver is a man with a tired face and labourer's hands. He looks at Lela's bloodstained mouth.

'What happened? Did someone do this to you?'

Lela starts crying in spite of herself. She wipes her dirty hands across her cheeks, rubs her eyes and screws up her face. She feels something lodge in her throat, choking her.

The man pulls over. He offers her a bottle of water.

'Hold out your hands for me and you can give your face a wash.'

Lela gets out and cups her hands. She splashes the water onto her face.

'A young girl like you shouldn't be out here alone,' the man says, when they're back in the car and heading down the road to Tbilisi. 'There are all sorts of bad people about… Are your parents still around?'

'Yes,' replies Lela.

'How old are you?'

'Eighteen.'

'Where do you live? I'll take you home.'

'Keep driving and I'll tell you the way.'

'What were you doing out here anyway?' asks the man.

A large lorry thunders past them with a deafening rumble, spewing thick black smoke.

'A friend took me for a drive,' Lela says. 'And then he drove off and left me there.'

'And did your friend do that too?' asks the man, without looking round. Lela glances at the man and is surprised to see deep, broken furrows running out from the corner of his eye to his temple.

He shakes his head.

Lela looks out of the window. The man's questions are making her tense.

By the time they drive into the city the light is fading fast. Lela recognizes her street, but sends the driver a different way and asks him to stop in front of a block of flats.

'Anywhere here will do. Thank you,' she says.

The man peers into the yard. There are children playing and a few young men hanging around. It's just an ordinary yard lit by the setting sun, with leafy shadows that embellish the tower block walls and a mother calling for her child from a top-floor window.

'Stop going off with people like that. There are too many weirdos out there,' says the man.

Lela gets out of the car and runs into the building that's not really hers.

*

Later that night, as Lela stands in the wash block, she is suddenly unnerved by the sound of gushing water echoing through the dark, deserted building.

She goes into the gatehouse. Through the darkness she can make out Irakli lying on her bed in a deep sleep. She gazes down at him. The moonlight is streaming onto his face. The Americans were right. His face is soft, his skin pale and almost translucent. He is breathing heavily. Lela sits down on the bed and takes off her shoes. She uses her back to shunt Irakli towards the wall. He squirms, then goes back to sleep. Lela can feel him breathing through her back. She remembers Koba, the five-*lari* note in her trouser pocket and the man with the deep creases round his eyes. She tries to think, but the thoughts fail to form in her head and soon Lela too is asleep.

The next day Lela goes round to the tower block next door. The yard is usually empty at this time of year: it's the summer holidays. The few children left behind sit at the table in the shade, playing cards and looking miserable. A group of young men including Koba and Goderdzi, who is getting ready for his second wedding, are hanging around nearby. This time Goderdzi isn't under his car; today they're watching Gocha wash his car with a hose. Lela goes over to the men and stands right in front of Koba. Koba is taken aback. The other men look on in astonishment. Lela pulls the five-*lari* note from her pocket and holds it out to Koba, who turns bright red.

'Here, you can take your five *lari* – I don't want it!' she says.

'Get lost, will you?' Koba hisses, raising his hand angrily and turning his back, before turning to face her again and muttering, 'Just piss off!'

The men laugh.

'What's going on? What does she want?' Gocha asks.

'Give it to me, love, if you don't want it,' sniggers one of the others.

'Give it to your grandmother and go fuck her instead,' says Lela, throwing the money at Koba's feet.

The others burst out laughing. Someone starts clapping. A man with a goatee snorts and says, 'Nice one!'

'You kept this quiet, Koba!' says a man in a denim waistcoat. 'God, you must have been desperate!'

'Come here, you bitch! You're fucking dead!' Koba shouts, and lunges at Lela. The other men hold him back as Lela starts walking away.

'Fucking nutjob!' shouts Koba.

Lela spins round.

'Don't you *ever* let me see that pile of rust in my yard again or I'll tell Tiniko about your five *lari*, and Piruz too, and then you're fucked, aren't you? Well and truly fucked by some nutjob, just like you wanted! So take your five *lari* and buy yourself something nice,' she spits, 'like your mother!'

'Steady on, love,' says a man with a smooth, deep voice. The other men hold Koba back. Gocha tries to turn the hose on Lela but the jet doesn't reach her. The guy in the waistcoat picks up a pebble and throws it hard at Lela's ankles.

'Leave her alone, man, she's a girl,' says the deep-voiced man.

An old man is looking out of one of the windows. Then a woman sticks her head out of another and asks angrily what's going on.

'Nothing, Mum. Go back in,' says the man with the goatee.

One evening when the light is fading, Koba bumps into Lela at the end of Kerch Street and punches her in the face. Lela falls to the ground and Koba kicks her repeatedly in the stomach and back. After that, he walks off and disappears from her life for ever.

8

August arrives. Time always passes slowly at the school, but now it seems to have stopped completely. The streets are empty; the air is still; even the dogs do as little as possible, shifting only to follow the creeping shade. There is no prospect of rain. There are no cool spells. Going outside is almost impossible. The sun blazes down from the moment it comes up, an enormous glowing ember mercilessly searing this side of the world. The ground is bone-dry, cracked like the top of a cake, and even the rust-coloured ants seem desperate, running frenetically across the scorching earth, looking for a crevice to shelter in and cool their tiny burnt feet.

In the evening when the sun goes down, the air still sits heavy. The moon casts shadows that transform the landscape. At last a hesitant breeze wafts in and the branches begin their gentle sway. The crickets chirp.

The children stagger around giddily in the heat. They don't want to play football. They don't want to eat. For some reason no one can fathom, Dali stops them playing with water to cool off. When nobody's looking, a few of them still manage to fill bottles with water and pour it all over their heads.

*

One evening when Dali and the children are hiding from the heat in the yard's shade, Father Yakob arrives wearing his black cassock and veil. Tariel's son, Gubaz, has taken a turn for the worse.

'I thought he usually got ill in the spring,' says Dali pensively.

'We've done everything we can. The doctor's been out too. It's up to God now,' says Father Yakob gravely. 'They even had Piruz round, but what on earth can he do? You can't throw someone in jail for being mentally ill.'

Piruz appears looking tired and anguished. Gubaz, he says, had chased his own parents round their vegetable garden with a hatchet.

'Thank goodness Kukura was there. He managed to catch him somehow and tied him up,' says Piruz. 'He took a couple of punches to the head, though… That's some right hook Gubaz has, uffff…' Piruz shakes his head. 'He can't go on like this. The boy needs medicine! He's OK one minute, like this the next… His parents had a lucky escape this time.'

'You're right,' Dali agrees. 'He's had bad spells before, but nothing like this. One time he started telling everyone he was God and walking around with eggs in his pockets. A few days later – right as rain…'

'You never know when it's coming. If only he was just feeble-minded like the little ones you have here,' says Piruz, wiping his forehead with a crumpled handkerchief.

'There's something else at play,' says Father Yakob. 'The Evil One spotted his weakness. He only needs the tiniest whisper of invitation. He knocks at your door and if you open it even an inch he comes right in and takes possession!'

'The Devil, Father?' Piruz asks, turning pale.

'Don't let his name pass your lips! Lord have mercy!' says the priest, making the sign of the cross. The others cross themselves too, three times.

'What is the cure, Father?' asks Dali anxiously.

'Prayer. Fasting. Vigilance. The Church and God's assistance,' he proclaims.

'Good Lord,' says Dali, as if she thinks this almost impossible.

'If curing madness were that simple there wouldn't be so many lunatics walking around,' says Avto, who has just come over. Avto gives Piruz and Vano brisk handshakes, then Father Yakob too. Clearly expecting a kiss on the hand, the priest narrows his eyes in disdain as Avto returns to his blue van.

Lela goes to open the gates. Piruz finishes his cigarette and heads off too.

Father Yakob frowns suddenly and looks at Dali.

'Do these children know how to pray?' he asks.

Taken aback, Dali seems unsure how to answer. The children stare at their feet awkwardly, embarrassed to be found wanting by a man of God.

'Teach them their prayers,' says Father Yakob sternly. He slips his hand into the pocket of the enormous canvas waistcoat he's wearing over his cassock and pulls out a couple of pamphlets. He hands one to Dali. 'Bedtime prayers. Make sure you teach them – you are their godmother, after all.'

Dali, red-faced, bows meekly, kisses Father Yakob's hand and takes the pamphlet.

One evening Lela wonders if bedtime prayers might have some merit after all, if they might chase away her strange, dreadful dreams. She finds Dali watching TV with the children.

'Dali, what did you do with that leaflet the priest gave you?'

Dali drags herself out of the armchair, goes over to a tatty shelf and pulls out the pamphlet.

'To be honest, I can't read it,' she says, flicking through the pages. 'I can't make any sense of formal prayers like this.'

Dali sits down in the armchair. Lela calls the children over. Dali pushes her glasses up her nose, stares down at the page for a while, then shuts the pamphlet and sets it aside. She looks at Pako and Stella, who are sitting right next to her.

'I was your age when my mother died,' she begins.

'Did you grow up in a school for slow children too?' Levan asks cheerfully. The children laugh, but Dali carries on.

'No, my grandmother raised me, God rest her soul.'

She looks up at the cobweb-covered ceiling and makes the sign of the cross. The children cross themselves earnestly too. Some kiss the crosses around their necks, as they have seen others do.

'I didn't know the first thing about praying or going to church – I grew up in the village. We did have a church, if you can call it that, up at the top of the hill, but it was so old… The roof had fallen in and there were trees growing inside the building. Just walls and a couple of icons really. My mother was so young when she had me. She was only twenty-one when she died. They used to take me there to light candles under the icons. At night my mum would put me to bed and say a little prayer. A children's prayer, though – a rhyme. After she died I'd say it with my grandmother instead. Even now, before I close my eyes, I say this prayer and I have no fear, for God is with me.'

The children hang on Dali's every word. Dali exhales deeply, then begins to recite:

'*Now I lay me down to sleep,*

I pray the Lord my soul to keep…'

When she comes to the end she wipes a tear from her eye. Vaska looks on from the doorway, a smile of slight disdain on his face.

All of a sudden, a strong breeze rushes in through the window and the heavens open. The children, jubilant, run to the window and thrust their hands into the cooling rain that spreads like a salve across the heat-scorched earth. The smell of wet asphalt fills the air.

'Ika, do they have rain in America?' asks Stella, trying to squeeze herself under Irakli's arm as he leans on the windowsill.

'Yeah, rain *and* hail. And storms. Haven't you seen their storms on TV? They have tornadoes so big they'll carry your whole house away!'

'Ika, no!' says Stella, covering her mouth with her hand. 'In that case don't go!'

That night Lela dreams she's back at the edge of the pear field. The children are playing football behind her. Lela runs out onto the field to fetch the ball but after a few steps she finds herself sinking into the soft, waterlogged earth. Suddenly the earth drags her in up to the waist. She reaches out to grab onto the gnarled roots. She tries to shout to the children but they're nowhere to be seen. She sinks deeper and deeper into the field.

The next morning Lela gets up early to let a few cars out, then goes to the dinner hall.

She doesn't like seeing the hall empty of children. The morning light is streaming through the windows and, where the dusty sunbeams fall, Lela can see bits of leftover bread on tables still not cleared from the night before, and glasses covered in fingerprints.

She goes to the cupboard and finds a piece of bread, spreads it with plum jam and eats it on her way out into the yard. None of the teachers are in yet and the children are all still asleep. A single hungry dog wanders through the spruce trees.

Tiniko arrives at work. Lela opens the gates and Tiniko click-clacks unsteadily across the yard in her wedge heels. Lela closes the gates behind her.

'Tiniko,' she says casually, 'I can't give you the parking money this month.'

Tiniko sits on the plank under the trees and pulls off her shoe to remove a stone. She frowns at Lela.

'Why not? Have you spent it?'

'I had to pay for a lot of things. For Irakli. I'll pay you next month.'

Tiniko says nothing. She squeezes her swollen foot back into her shoe and stands up.

'Tell me he's learning something at least,' she says.

'Yeah, he's learning,' Lela replies with a shrug.

'Don't go to too much trouble, all right? Nobody's expecting him to be fluent. You need to look after things here. He'll be gone soon but you'll still be here and these cars are your responsibility. You understand what responsibility is, right? I'm counting on you, you know that.'

'I know, Tiniko.'

After lunch, Marika arrives with a new batch of swear words. Irakli is especially pleased with *You bastard!* and *I'll kill you!* Lela can't give Marika the twenty *lari* she'd promised, nor the five *lari* for this week. Marika doesn't pressure her; as August is nearly over, she agrees to let Lela pay her back with the parking money she collects in September and then they'll be quits.

With the arrival of autumn, the whole school comes alive. They tidy the yard and fix the broken fence, and Tiniko even brings some paint from her house so that Avto can paint the main gates green and the front door maroon.

They clean inside the main building too. Dali gets down on her knees to scrub the floor with laundry soap and an old shoe brush before the children apply a layer of polish.

In the TV room they do the best they can. A couple of the teachers bring in potted aloes and roses from home. Avto and Vano drag the sofa out into the yard and Tiniko gets the children to beat it with sticks to remove all the dust, then relocates it to her office and covers it with an old bedspread with a sinister-looking tiger motif.

Goderdzi's wedding is to take place in September, so the entrance to the dinner hall gets a new coat of paint too. Venera pays for this herself, along with some minor repairs inside the dinner hall. The holes where nails have held up countless flags and pictures over the years are filled in with plaster and sanded down, and the walls and windowsills are painted white. All traces of the past are removed. Avto insists that the old paint needs to be sanded before the new paint goes on, but Venera wants things done as quickly and cheaply as possible. She hopes this will be Goderdzi's last wedding and that she won't ever have to worry about the state of the dinner hall again.

Teachers and children alike approach the renovations with a sense of great pride because they are also due to host two extremely important guests from America: Irakli's new parents, Deborah and John.

When the big day arrives, Lela throws open the green school gates and a cream-coloured Volga sedan drives in carrying

Madonna, Deborah, John and Shalva, the driver, who is somehow related to Madonna.

While the furore surrounding the Americans' stay is not as great as that once created by Marcel's arrival, everyone is beside themselves with excitement nonetheless, because this visit confirms that there is indeed a world outside Georgia, Tbilisi and Kerch Street.

The welcome ceremony takes place in the gymnasium. The assembly hall has been off-limits for years. Velvet curtains have been brought over from the assembly hall and hung on the gym's wall-mounted exercise bars. Benches have been set out to form three sides of a makeshift stage.

The children file cautiously into the gym. Every child still harbours the memory of their friend and brother Sergo laid out on the desk in the middle of the hall.

Deborah and John are led into the gymnasium by Tiniko and Madonna. Dali marches in behind them. The strange, acrid smell of washing powder is almost overpowering.

The second the Americans appear the children fall silent.

'*Hello, everybody!*' John calls out, raising his hand to greet them. His voice is smooth and melodious. The children freeze.

They see a tall man of average build, whose body seems to be sagging in places and who is carrying a little extra padding on the hips. His smile is so pure and sincere that it's hard to imagine he has ever been happier than at this moment. Everyone stares as he walks over to the stage.

'*Hello, everybody! How's everyone doing today?*' he bellows cheerfully.

For some reason, Gulnara starts clapping. The children join in. Madonna hisses, 'Stop clapping, you'll scare them off – I mean, they know where they are but still, let's try to rein it in a bit, shall we?'

She turns back to the children.

'John is asking you how you are. He wants to know if you're all OK.'

'We're fi-i-i-ne,' a few children call out timidly.

Deborah is standing next to John, smiling broadly. With her ample hips and slender trunk she looks like a good-natured pot plant. She starts speaking and Madonna translates into Georgian: 'Although we have come here for Irakli, we think of you all as members of our family and we want you all to grow up to be strong, capable adults. Unfortunately, we can only adopt one child, but we want you to know you are all in our hearts. You're Irakli's brothers and sisters, after all!'

'Pff, his brother? No thank you!' exclaims Levan loudly.

The children burst out laughing. Deborah is confused, but tries to gather her thoughts and finish what she was saying. Tiniko whispers to Lela, who turns to Levan sitting behind her and tells him to follow Tiniko outside. While Deborah carries on with her speech, Tiniko strides briskly out of the gym with Levan slumping along behind her, like a prisoner about to face the firing squad, except that Levan has faced the firing squad before.

Levan has barely stepped outside when Tiniko closes the door and grabs him by the earlobe.

'Why can't you just behave?' she hisses so that nobody

in the hall will hear. Levan grimaces and lets out a moan. Tiniko digs her painted nails harder into his ear and twists it as if she's opening a tap.

'Hush! I don't want to hear another peep out of you!'

Levan gives a pitiful croak. Tiniko lets go. Levan tries to run off, but Tiniko pounces like a hungry animal. As she raises her hand, her ill-fitting costume ring rotates on her finger and when she brings her hand back down to slap Levan hard across the back, she catches his spine with the gemstone. Levan screams and darts forward like a shot deer.

'I'm going to put you six feet under, boy!' spits Tiniko. 'Next time your mum visits you it'll be in the graveyard!'

Levan doesn't hear. He is already halfway across the empty yard. His face is red and his ear is still smarting. He would cry, but the tears won't come. He feels the sharp pain in his ear gradually ebbing. A dog hobbles across the yard and in the street a bus rattles past belching thick black smoke.

When Tiniko goes back inside, Shalva is carrying a couple of large sacks onto the stage. Deborah opens them and explains that these are presents – clothes, shoes and toys – that her neighbours have sent for the children. Tiniko tells Dali and Avto to keep the sacks for now and takes Deborah and John out of the hall, along with Madonna, Irakli and Lela.

They gather in Tiniko's office. Dali brings in some instant coffee and honey biscuits.

As soon as they walk in, Deborah throws her arms open and says, *'Now we're alone I can hug Irakli!'*

Deborah and John both hug him tightly. Dali watches out of the corner of her eye while she's pouring the coffee and her eyes fill with tears again. Irakli is blushing furiously. He has no idea why Deborah keeps looking him straight in the eye and speaking English as if he was already an American. Maybe they think he understands what they're saying. Maybe they'll be upset when they find out the truth.

Then Madonna translates: 'She says they've been waiting a long time for this day. They are so happy you're going to live with them. Their children are adults now and have their own places so you'll be the only child. She hopes it won't be too dull for you. But she says they have a big family close by and they also have two grandchildren.'

Deborah laughs and says something else. Irakli stands there, as stiff as a board and sweating nervously while Madonna translates: 'Basically, she's saying you've got all the time in the world to get to know each other properly.'

John smiles warmly at Irakli and asks, 'What do you think? Do you want to come and see America?'

Irakli nods.

Deborah and John want to see every inch of the school; it will help them understand Irakli better. Tiniko and Madonna lead them off on a tour. Irakli and Lela go back outside and are immediately surrounded by a large group of children desperate to hear every detail.

The next day Madonna takes Deborah and John to see Tbilisi. They take Irakli too, so that they can get to know each other better. Irakli seems disorientated. He wants Lela to come, but nobody invites her.

Later that evening Lela goes out to the deserted playground. Irakli still isn't back. Lela climbs the iron staircase right up to the top. She sits on the top step and lights a cigarette. She sees Deborah and John flash before her eyes, then Irakli, beetroot-red, then Vano as she lures him into the trampoline room and out onto the edge of the collapsed balcony and pushes...

Can you do it? asks a voice in her head. *Can you? Then what the hell are you waiting for?*

I'll kill him before the end of winter. Once Irakli's gone, I'll do it, replies Lela.

It's still dusk when, back in the gatehouse, Lela falls into a deep sleep.

The door opens and Irakli comes in. Lela wakes up. Irakli comes over to the bed and perches, feather-light, on the edge.

'Tell me what you've been doing, then,' Lela says.

Irakli doesn't reply. Lela studies his face in the moonlight streaming through the gatehouse window. There's something strange about how he looks and he is oddly silent.

'What's up with you?'

Irakli says nothing.

'What's the matter?' Lela gives him a shake.

Irakli grimaces and tries to break free.

'My stomach,' he mumbles.

Lela lets go and stands up. She twists the bulb and a yellow light fills the room. Irakli is hunched up on the bed, moaning.

'What's wrong? What did you eat?'

'*Khinkali*,' he moans. 'Too many.'

Lela thinks for a minute.

'Are they not sitting well?'

'And *shashlik*... and *lobiani*...'

'Was there something wrong with it?'

'It was all fine...' He groans again.

'Did you eat too much?'

'Yeah,' says Irakli, starting to cry. 'I feel sick...'

'Come on, get up. It's not sitting well and you need to throw up,' says Lela, helping him to his feet.

Lela takes him into the toilets in the main building. The smell is so pungent that Irakli vomits as soon as he walks in, sending an array of Georgian delicacies straight down the sewer pipe. He collapses onto the sink, tears streaming down his face, throat burning. Lela turns on the tap and the water comes out so fast it splashes their fronts. Still trembling, Irakli washes his face.

'It hasn't helped,' says Irakli when they go outside.

'Look, you're leaving for America in two days. Stop blubbing over a couple of dumplings!'

Khatuna, a young trainee from Rustavi, walks across from the dinner hall, carrying a cup of tea for Irakli.

'I don't want it,' Irakli says, flapping his hands and talking as if he can't move his tongue properly.

'Where do you want to lie down, in mine or upstairs?' asks Lela.

'Yours,' he answers, and follows her to the gatehouse.

They go inside. Khatuna sets the tea down and puts her hand on Irakli's forehead while he lies on the bed groaning.

'Go to sleep. You'll feel better when you wake up,' says Khatuna, adding, 'Should I call Tiniko or Dali, do you think?'

'No, he'll be fine,' says Lela. 'He just ate a bit too much. His stomach's not used to the good life.'

They laugh. Irakli screws himself up in a ball on the bed.

'Where will you sleep?' asks Khatuna.

'I'll just perch on the edge. It's only for two days and then off he goes to America!' Lela says, rooting around to find Irakli's arms and giving him a shake. Irakli moans.

Khatuna leaves. Lela turns the light off and lies down next to Irakli with her head at the opposite end of the bed.

They lie in silence for a while. Lela's eyes adjust to the darkness. She watches the room slowly take form: Tariel's cut-glass ashtray glints in the moonlight, the contours of the mirror emerge and the cross Lela pinned to the frame casts a forbidding shadow across the wall. Irakli is breathing unevenly and Lela knows he is not asleep.

'Hey!' she says, giving him a sharp kick. 'Tell me where you went.'

Irakli squirms, rolls onto his back, but makes no sound other than a moan of discomfort.

'Hey! Did you vomit your voice box out too?' says Lela, feeling around for Irakli's face with her foot.

'Shove off, will you!' Irakli croaks.

'I want to know where you went!'

'We went to look at stuff...'

'Did you go to a restaurant?'

'Yeah.'

'What did you eat?'

'Oh God, can we not talk about food?'

'Fine. At least tell me what you saw.'

'We went round Tbilisi, then out to Mtskheta.'

'Is it far?'

'Yeah.'

'And? What else? Did you speak English?'

'Yeah, I said *OK* and *no*.'

For a while neither says anything.

'In Mtskheta there was this church and some priests. And there were some statues... We saw a man on a horse carrying a sword...'

'A statue, you mean?'

'Yeah. He was sitting on a big horse and if you stood right underneath you could see these massive balls.'

'What, on the man or the horse?' laughs Lela.

'The horse.'

'What about his willy?'

'Couldn't see,' answers Irakli.

'What's Mtskheta like?'

'Good.'

'How many *khinkali* did you eat?'

'Lela, don't... I still feel sick.'

Lela takes her cigarettes out of the drawer.

'What did the Americans say?'

'I dunno. Nothing much.'

Lela gets up and goes outside to smoke. When she comes back in, Irakli is asleep.

The neighbourhood women can barely conceal their disappointment. Goderdzi's new bride is nothing like Manana. Irma doesn't smile like Manana or sway her hips like Manana or, in fact, do anything suggestive of loose morals whatsoever. They struggle to find anything in Irma's life to criticize at all. Her respectability is stultifying.

Goderdzi looks happy enough, although he has shaved so enthusiastically that his face has gone red and puffy.

Nobody seems to know who the toastmaster is this time. He is a tiny self-deprecating man with an expression of mild irritation. He manages to poke fun at himself in his toasts – 'Gentlemen, please be upstanding, although I will stay seated as it makes no real difference...' – which the guests take as evidence of true magnanimity.

Once again, Goderdzi's cousin is attending with his revolver tucked into his belt. He seems out of sorts. In fact, the entire wedding party seem slightly subdued, as if they are all missing Manana, the woman who by rights should never have married a man like Goderdzi but did so anyway. Nothing would ever top that.

Irma is wearing a simple white satin dress and sits next to Goderdzi, smiling shyly. She looks more embarrassed than happy. Her mother is not at the table; instead, she is helping the serving staff. It seems reasonable to assume that the minute Irma walks into Venera and Goderdzi's home she will take off her white wedding dress, take up the yoke of domestic duties and work like a mule until her dying breath.

The children's table is laid out in a corner of the dinner hall. As guests of honour, John and Deborah are offered prime position at the top table, but they choose instead to join the children. Dali, who had been about to start eating a piece of fish with her fingers, is confused to discover such esteemed guests suddenly sitting opposite. Her appetite disappears. Dali can only marvel at Madonna's ability to eat in front of the Americans with such single-minded focus while simultaneously holding her own in a foreign language.

The *duduki* players come out onto the dance floor and the drum strikes up a steady rhythm. A handful of young women in traditional dresses start to dance. A few minutes later a young man leaps onto the dance floor with his arms outstretched, dances a large circle around the young women and then takes a position right in the middle, scattering the women like a flock of startled hens. Deborah and John stare, transfixed. John is almost moved to tears. Their happiness is tinged with slight unease, with a sense of regret about taking Irakli, their chosen son, from this magical fairy-tale country to a place where nobody, even at a wedding, could ever dance with such passion.

9

The day of Irakli's departure arrives.

Lela crosses herself in front of the mirror before she leaves the gatehouse.

Irakli is standing by the gates with the small black suitcase Deborah and John gave him. Around his neck hangs a small cloth wallet with an airline logo on the front and his passport inside.

The whole school is gathered at the gates.

Irakli leafs through his brand-new passport while the others look on. He examines each blank page carefully. Finally he reaches the page with his American visa and photo. Irakli lets Stella hold the passport so she can have a closer look. She stares at the visa and then turns to the last page to look at Irakli's photo. Suddenly Levan grabs at the passport. Stella, holding on tight, yanks her hand back and howls, glaring at Levan so hard that the sinews in her neck stick out.

'You'll rip it!' she cries, her face turning a deep red. She raises her arm high in the air and searches wide-eyed for Irakli in the crowd.

'Give it to him,' he says reassuringly.

Still angry, Stella gives the burgundy passport to Levan. He opens it carefully, like a love letter, and stares at it.

'Well then, Irakli, look after yourself,' Dali says, walking towards the children with Tiniko, Madonna, Deborah and John. Levan gives the passport back and asks Irakli to send him a gun from America.

Stella hugs Irakli fiercely. Vaska comes over and shakes Irakli's hand vigorously. Dali hugs him next. She is crying.

'We've never sent anyone this far away before,' she says between sobs.

'We have, Dali!' Levan chimes in. 'We sent Sergo all the way to heaven, God rest his soul…'

'I'll deal with you later,' Tiniko says.

John takes a group photo of the children with Irakli in the middle. Everyone wants to stand next to him.

Marika comes into the yard looking tanned and freckly after her holiday. She is wearing a short yellow dress and her hair is loose. The sight of a smiling Marika so skimpily dressed makes Levan freeze on the spot.

Marika has brought Irakli a small English dictionary as a present.

'*Dick*-tionary!' Irakli says, smiling.

Shalva starts the car. Zaira comes hurrying over with a plastic bag of sweets from her kiosk. She hands them out to the children before pulling Irakli into a tight hug.

'Don't forget us, Irakli!'

Tiniko's husband, Temur, pulls up behind the wheel of a foreign car. He is a thin, bald man with a flat broken nose and a sincere smile. His skin has the pallor of a heavy smoker and every few seconds he lifts his fist to his mouth and coughs violently. Tiniko tells everybody to get in.

It's swelteringly hot. Tiniko winds the window down and fans her face with her hands. The cars drive off, leaving Dali standing by the school gates surrounded by her waving godchildren.

Irakli rolls his window down and turns his face into the wind. Tiniko and Temur are talking in the front, but Lela can't hear what they're saying over the noise of the engine. She looks out of the window. She pretends that she's the one going to America and leaving for good, leaving the school, Dali, the children and all her teachers, leaving Zaira and her kiosk, the neighbours in the block next door, Marika, Koba, Goderdzi and his new wife, Irma. The car turns out of Kerch Street and Lela says goodbye to her old life for ever.

Irakli is wearing a smart dark blue shirt buttoned up to his neck, jeans held up by a red elasticated belt, and boots from the bag of clothes Deborah and John brought with them. He sits in silence, looking calm, content and, Lela thinks, older. He points out familiar streets and buildings.

'I've seen that one before…'

Lela gazes out of the window absent-mindedly.

When I get back from the airport I'm going to kill Vano, she thinks. *Then I'm getting out of here, just like the others did.*

She imagines herself finding Yana and following her into her one-room flat. *Even if they arrest me*, she thinks, *they'll let me out before long, or maybe send me to the madhouse…* Lela thinks about Yana again, but when she was younger, when she moved out of the school, dressed in that checked shirt done up to the neck. Yana smiles. Her flat is like Mzia's, with the smell of fresh baking and a sideboard in the hall, and the apron she is wearing is just like Mzia's too. 'Come with me,' Yana says. They leave the flat and go outside to work. Lela is so happy her feet hardly touch the pavement…

Then she remembers that Irakli is going to America and all thoughts of Yana fly out of her head.

They arrive at the airport. As they are getting out of the car Irakli tells Lela that his head hurts and he feels sick, but both of them know there isn't time for him to be ill.

Standing in the queue at check-in, Irakli turns to Lela.

'I still feel sick,' he says.

'You'll feel better in a minute,' says Lela.

Madonna overhears and tells John.

John disappears somewhere with Irakli. A few minutes later they come back with a large packet of chewing gum. Irakli takes the sticks out and offers them round. The women take a stick each.

Once they've checked in John invites everybody to the airport's only café. Temur sees one of his relatives and wanders off for a chat. Shalva also declines.

The waiter pushes two tables together and slaps a couple of menus down in front of them. John orders coffees, some juice and a selection of cakes and sandwiches.

'You don't look very happy,' Lela says to Irakli, who is picking unenthusiastically at a cream cake.

'I'm not,' says Irakli quietly.

'Sure,' laughs Lela, and cuffs him hard on the back of the head, knocking his nose into his cream cake. Madonna and Tiniko laugh loudly, but John glances disapprovingly at Lela like a father whose child is misbehaving.

After they leave the café they go to the escalators to see Irakli off. John and Deborah hug Tiniko and Lela, and shake hands with Temur and Shalva. Tiniko throws her arms around Irakli, fighting back tears and trying to make their hug last as long as possible. Madonna hugs him next. Temur puts his hand on Irakli's shoulder and smiles at him warmly.

Irakli and Lela give each other a quick, tearless, silent hug.

John wheels Irakli's small black cabin bag onto the escalator and turns to wave back at everyone. Irakli and Deborah get on behind him and the three of them travel slowly upwards.

They are almost at the top when Irakli suddenly breaks away from Deborah and starts walking quickly back down the escalator.

'Irakli! Irakli!' Deborah calls out anxiously. '*John, do something!*'

Deborah stands there helplessly watching Irakli weave in and out of his fellow passengers, one of whom has her bag knocked out of her hands. When he reaches the bottom he jumps off, dodges Tiniko and the others and speeds away across the terminal.

'I think he's feeling sick,' says Lela, and goes after him.

The Americans get on the escalator back to the ground floor. Tiniko, Madonna and Temur meet them at the bottom. John is red in the face and looks offended. Deborah is deadly pale and flustered.

'I think he's gone to the toilet to be sick,' Tiniko says, as Madonna translates. 'It's probably nerves.'

'Let's move to one side, shall we? We're in the way here,' says Temur.

Shalva appears and speaks for the first time that day: now is his moment for chivalry.

'I'll go and find them,' he says, hitching his trousers up and disappearing off into the crowd.

Lela finds Irakli standing by the entrance to the toilets staring vacantly.

'Are you out of your mind?'

Irakli says nothing.

'Did you throw up?'

'No,' says Irakli.

'What did you run off for, then? You almost gave them a heart attack! Don't start acting like an idiot now.'

Lela shoves him back against the wall and looks him in the eye.

'Now get back over there and do your best *I am sorry* for your... parents, do you hear me?'

Irakli says nothing.

'Boy, do you hear me? Either go and throw up, or get your arse back over there right now!'

'I don't want to go to America,' Irakli says in a pitiful voice. He screws his face up but the tears lodge in his throat and turn to bile.

Lela raises her hand and slaps Irakli hard across the face.

He falls back against the wall, sinks down onto his knees and starts to cry. John appears out of nowhere, grabs Lela by the arm and spins her round. He looks like a different man. The kind face and warm smile are gone. He shakes Lela and shouts at her in English.

'What does he want from me?' Lela asks Madonna, who is trying her best to calm John down.

John lets go of Lela's arm and explains that Lela slapped Irakli, then turns to Tiniko and jabs his finger in her face as if he's somehow blaming her.

Tiniko goes red. Suddenly her patience runs out. She thrusts her jaw forward and shouts at John in Georgian, 'I said it was a bad idea, sending one as old as Irakli, but nobody listened, did they!'

Deborah goes to Irakli, who is sitting on the floor with his head between his knees.

'Irakli,' she says, gently putting her hand on his arm and lowering herself awkwardly to her knees.

Deborah beckons Madonna over. Unable to kneel because of her size, Madonna stays standing to translate.

'Irakli, she's asking what's wrong. Don't be embarrassed if you're feeling sick. It doesn't matter, she says. Just go into the toilets and do what you need to. Then come back out and have a bit of a rest… If you want, she says Lela can take you outside for some fresh air. She says there's plenty of time.'

Irakli lifts his head. His eyes are red and his face tear-stained. He looks at Deborah and shouts, 'I don't want to go to America! I don't want to go!'

Madonna stands there, numb. Deborah looks up and waits, chin trembling, for her to translate.

'*What did he say? What did he say about America?*'

'*Nothing!*' says Madonna firmly, then screams down at Irakli, 'Don't push me, young man! Do *not* show me up in front of these people. Just shut up, stand up and go with this lady, that's all we're asking of you! Just get in the plane and when you get to the other end there'll be a whole new life waiting for you, a *good* life... Everything you could possibly want. But they are not going to take you if you keep kicking up a fuss like this...'

Irakli stands up, opens the wallet round his neck and throws his passport onto the floor as if he's slapping an ace on the table. He walks off without a word.

'*What did he say? Doesn't he want to come with us?*' asks Deborah again.

Temur helps Deborah to her feet. Tiniko notices her husband begin to stroke Deborah's pale, soft hand. She marches over, pulls Deborah aside and glowers at Temur.

'We'll sort it out, Deborah,' Tiniko says in Georgian. 'Don't worry, he's just a stupid child. What does he know about America?'

She grits her teeth, clenches her fist in front of her face and glares at her husband. Temur shrugs and steps to one side awkwardly.

Irakli is still striding across the terminal. Lela, Madonna, Tiniko and Deborah start after him, but John blocks their path.

'Let me go,' he says earnestly.

'Irakli,' he says, catching up and taking Irakli gently by the elbow. Irakli shrugs him off.

'*Irakli, we'll do whatever you want. It's OK if you don't want to come with us. We won't be angry. It's up to you.*'

Madonna follows behind in a weak jog, weaving through the crowds as she translates.

John puts his hand back on Irakli's elbow and turns him around. He looks at him warmly and gives a calm, kind smile.

Irakli pulls his arm free and screams, '*Fuck you, bastard! I kill you! I kill you!*'

The smile on John's face vanishes. At first he isn't sure he has heard correctly. The others finally catch up with them. Irakli stands some distance apart, as if facing down a pack of snarling hounds.

'*Fuck you, old bastard! I kill you! I kill you! Don't touch me!*' Irakli screams at John again, and Lela suddenly remembers Irakli jumping on the bed bases in the summer rain.

Without warning, Deborah faints. Temur grabs her as she falls and is pulled to the ground along with her. John runs over.

'Deborah! Deborah!' he cries, white as a sheet.

Shalva and Madonna try to lift Deborah to her feet while Temur flails underneath her. A woman runs over with a bottle of water, kneels next to Deborah and rubs her forehead and temples with calloused hands. Deborah's eyes open.

'Is she a foreigner?' the woman asks with a slow, provincial cadence.

'Oh my goodness!' groans Madonna. 'My poor nerves… Yes, she's a foreigner.'

'Probably exhaustion. Take her outside so she can get some fresh air in her lungs,' says the woman.

'Where the hell is she going to find fresh air round here? We're not in the mountains now!' says a man, presumably the woman's husband. 'They probably gave her too much to drink and she can't handle it…'

They help Deborah onto a seat. John holds Deborah's hand and whispers in her ear.

Lela stands off to one side watching closely. Although the snarling hounds have dispersed, Irakli is still rooted to the spot.

A voice over the Tannoy announces that John and Deborah Sheriff and Irakli Tskhadadze should report to the departure gate immediately. John helps Deborah to her feet and they make their way to the escalator. The other adults follow, Madonna apologizing in English and Tiniko in Georgian. Temur apologizes in Russian for good measure and watches sadly as Deborah gets ready to leave.

At the escalator John stops to say a final farewell to his hosts. This time there are no handshakes or embraces. John thanks Tiniko and Madonna. He says they should have spent longer in Georgia getting to know Irakli, but that it would probably be better for everyone this way.

Tiniko feels someone pull on her arm. It's Lela.

'We're gonna go. We'll make our own way back.' She looks at Deborah and John, standing mutely by the escalator. With unexpected sincerity, she says, '*Goodbye, John. Goodbye, Deborah.*'

Lela and Irakli walk out of the airport and pick up a taxi.

'No luggage?'

'No,' says Lela. 'Can you take us to Kerch Street?'

'That'll cost you fifteen *lari*.'

'I know. We can pay.'

Lela and Irakli sit in silence in the back. Lela can tell he's crying. The driver is playing Georgian love songs on the radio and they gradually lose themselves in the intoxicating melodies.

Irakli leans over towards Lela to say something. The music is so loud that he has to shout.

'Do you think they put my suitcase on the plane?'

Lela is suddenly furious.

'Do you know what? You and your suitcase can both fuck right off!'

Irakli says nothing. He presses his pale face against the window and stares at the trees lining the road, wishing he could turn everything over to them, the swearing, the anger, his stupid suitcase and the America he would now never see, and watch as they whizzed past and carried it all far away.

Lela asks the driver to pull over by a roadside kiosk some distance away from Kerch Street.

'Could you wait here for a minute while I get some chewing gum for my friend? He's feeling a bit sick.'

The man pulls over.

'Wait here and I'll bring you some,' Lela says to Irakli.

Irakli knows what's coming.

The driver turns off the engine, pulls out a cleaning cloth and starts polishing the inside of the windscreen while he waits.

Irakli's heart is pounding. He puts one hand on the door handle and stares at the back of the driver's neck, at his broad shoulders, his strong, rough hands and fingernails blackened by hours spent fiddling with car parts. The driver folds the cloth and leans over to put it back where it came from and at that precise moment Irakli opens the door.

They run as fast as they can and they don't look back.

They don't stop until they're a long way away. There's no sign of the taxi driver. They don't even know whether he bothered giving chase at all.

They spot a row of kiosks nearby. Lela buys a Coke and they carry on walking.

'Is Tiniko going to beat me?' asks Irakli.

'She's not allowed to,' says Lela.

'What about you? Are you going to beat me?'

Lela hands him the bottle of Coke.

'It's what you deserve. But what good would it do? It's not like it would knock any sense into you.'

Irakli puts the empty bottle in his pocket.

'There's no deposit back on that one,' says Lela.

Irakli takes the bottle back out of his pocket and throws it onto a dusty grass verge.

Lela stops at the crossroads.

'We're near the cemetery.'

'What, where Sergo's buried?'

'No, my aunt Shushana. Yes, where Sergo's buried! Come on, let's go and visit his grave.'

They buy a small, slightly wilted posy of yellow wildflowers from an elderly lady for twenty *tetri*. She looks like one of her flowers: her small, delicate face is covered in wrinkles and she is wearing a flowery yellow headscarf.

The closer they get to the cemetery, the harder it is to work out which entrance they need. More than once they have to turn back from an entrance because Sergo's grave will be impossible to access from that side of the cemetery.

Irakli trudges wearily next to Lela. The flowers are making his palm sweat. Lela stops a man in the street.

'Can we get into the cemetery round here?' asks Lela.

'The cemetery? Yes, you can. If you go up that path –'

'No, no,' interrupts Lela. 'We went up that way just now. We're looking for one of the other entrances. We were here a few months back. It's near a tower block that's half gutted, but there are people still living in the other half. The whole thing's sinking into the earth.'

'Oh, you mean the Titanic! You need to go up that way. Go past two tower blocks and you'll see the road surface suddenly gets really bad. As soon as the road gets bad you need to head up the hill and keep going till you hit a huge patch of mud. You go round that and you'll come out in the yard right in front of the Titanic!'

*

Walking through the cemetery, Lela looks at the head-stones.

'He hasn't got a headstone,' she says, 'but I remember they buried him next to a Neli Aivazova or something like that. Keep an eye out for her.'

It's dusk and the last mourners are making their way out. Lela and Irakli remain inside, walking around, unable to find either Sergo or Neli Aivazova.

'She had a black headstone with her picture etched on. She was laughing and she looked a bit like Dali,' says Lela.

They sit down for a rest next to a long-neglected grave with a rusting iron fence and a thick covering of weeds. Lela stares at the listing tower block at the edge of the cemetery where she can already see lights in the windows.

'Lela,' says Irakli, 'my mum isn't coming back, is she? That's why Tiniko wanted to send me to America.'

Lela thinks about Irakli's mother, Inga, and the old Greek woman's words – '*Inga no live here any more!*' – and it all seems a very long time ago.

'You never know,' replies Lela. 'Anything's possible.'

'Do you really think so?' Irakli asks in surprise.

'I'm leaving,' Lela says suddenly. 'Leaving the school, I mean. But don't tell anyone. There's something I need to take care of, but once that's done I'll be off.'

'Where are you going?' Irakli asks resentfully.

'I don't know yet. Somewhere.'

Irakli gets to his feet and looks at Lela as if he's just been abandoned for the second time.

'If you keep your mouth shut and give me a hand, I'll take you with me,' says Lela casually. 'You don't deserve it, but what can I do?' Then, remembering what they're there for, she says, 'Go round to the other side of that hill and see if she's buried round there. Find her and we find Sergo.'

Irakli glances down at his wilting flowers, embarrassed to be taking Sergo such a pitiful offering.

'Lela,' says Irakli, 'maybe you've remembered it wrong. Try and think. Maybe it wasn't Neli Aivazova…'

'I dunno. It was a woman, she was laughing and the headstone was black. And she looked a bit like Dali.'

Irakli looks out over the cemetery, but nothing seems familiar.

A dog comes winding its way through the gravestones, head hanging down, swaying its thin haunches. They stare in surprise to see a living creature moving with such nonchalance through this bleak setting.

'Let's go back to the school,' says Lela. She turns, fixes the Titanic in her sights and plots their route out of the cemetery.

Irakli looks at the gravestones. He leaves the flowers with Izabela Gegechkori, whose grave has no portrait, candle or offerings.

'We didn't find Sergo,' he says dolefully.

'No,' says Lela.

At the end of Kerch Street they bump into Vaska sitting on an open concrete pipe by the bus stop, smoking a cigarette.

'Gimme a smoke,' Lela asks.

Vaska takes a full packet of cigarettes out of his pocket and holds it out to her.

'Wow, check you out!' she says.

'Take a few,' says Vaska, and looks at Irakli. 'You didn't go to America, then?'

'No,' says Irakli. 'Who told you?'

'Tiniko's back. And she's told Dali. Dali wants to give you a beating.'

'Does she want to give his mum a beating too?' says Lela. Vaska's smile widens.

Lela and Irakli walk on towards the school.

'Did you see his bag?' Irakli asks.

Lela doesn't remember seeing a bag.

'So what?'

'I think he's off.'

'Off where?'

'Just off. Leaving.'

Lela scoffs and spits to one side.

'He can go, then.'

'Lela, you won't let them beat me, will you?'

'If anyone's going to beat you it'll be me. Anyone else can mind their own business.'

Irakli takes a drag on the cigarette and feels his head become pleasantly dizzy. As they approach the school gates, Lela imagines them walking into the yard, the children and teachers crowding around them and all the ensuing commotion. Irakli's heart is in his mouth. Lela feels an unpleasant taste rise in her throat.

'Just stay right next to me,' she hisses at Irakli under her breath.

When they reach the gates they see Kolya and a couple of other children running across the yard. The children notice Lela and Irakli but ignore them completely and sprint past.

They walk into the yard and spot Levan. He too sees them but keeps running.

They watch Pako and Stella come running from the direction of the playground. Pako is out in front, with Stella hurrying behind as best she can in flip-flops. They race towards the dinner hall, but when they see children streaming out towards them with Dali close behind, they turn and run back towards the playground.

Pako shouts to Lela and Irakli, 'Vano was in the trampoline room. He fell!'

Pako's eyes are as wide as those of the Mickey Mouse on his T-shirt.

Irakli abandons all thoughts of America and races after the others.

For a moment Lela just stands there, unable to move. Her whole body is suddenly weightless. She sits down on the bench between the spruce trees. Rests her head on the trunk. Closes her eyes. There in the darkness she sees Vaska's face, and he's smiling.

Subscribe

Discover the best of contemporary European literature: subscribe to Peirene Press and receive a world-class novella from us three times a year, direct to your door. The books are sent out six weeks before they are available in bookshops and online.

Your subscription will allow us to plan ahead with confidence and help us to continue to introduce English readers to the joy of new foreign literature for many years to come.

'A class act'
THE GUARDIAN

'Two-hour books to be devoured in a single sitting: literary cinema for those fatigued by film'
TIMES LITERARY SUPPLEMENT

A one year subscription costs £35 (3 books, free p&p for UK)

Please sign up via our online shop at www.peirenepress.com/shop

2021
Peirene STEVNS
TRANSLATION PRIZE

The Peirene Stevns Translation Prize was launched in 2018 to support up-and-coming translators.

Open to all translators without a published novel, this prize looks not only to award great translation but also to offer new ways of entry into the world of professional translation. The winner receives a £3,500 commission to translate a text selected by Peirene Press, the opportunity to spend two months at a retreat in the Pyrenees and a dedicated one-on-one mentorship throughout the translation process.

The Peirene Stevns Prize focuses on a different language each year and is open for submissions from October to January.

With thanks to Martha Stevns, without whom this prize would not be possible.